CALI

V. ANGELO

To my family.
Thank you for always supporting me.

To my husband. You're my favorite.

To anyone who has lost someone dear.
Time may pass, but the grief never does.

cry (krī)

verb

A state of sadness – *cry when you are melancholy*

sorrow

A state of frustration or anger – *cry when you are mad*

heartache

A state of grief – *cry when you are mourning*

devastation

A state of shedding tears – *cry from your eyes*

happiness

V. ANGELO

"That was a mighty fall you three had." The woman opens her eyes looking to Jejune, Stevey, and I laying before her in pain. She retracts her arms and gently smiles at us. "The momentum from the hill really flung you. Will you be needing medical assistance?" None of us answer. With much effort, I begin to peel myself off the dusty ground.

The woman reaches down to help, her beaded necklaces clanking as she extends her hand. Jejune refuses, turning to Stevey to help him. I, unlike Jejune, politely decline, slowly hoisting myself up.

"Come," the woman says. She gives us one last look with her large doe eyes, haunting with the black makeup smeared all around. Looking to Jejune for reassurance, she nods, holding Stevey extremely close as she walks behind the woman's flowing attire.

As my body silently screams in agony, I too follow our guide. Her mermaid long hair blows with the wind, the petals on her head wavering slightly. Rubbing a knot out of my shoulder, I take in our surroundings. Just like our fall to land here, the view before us is breathtaking.

Turquoise spreads across the sky as the day transforms to evening. Blinding, the sun reflects off the pebble gray trailers lightly dusted with sand. Further up, my eyes move to see hills of greenery. Desert, gardens, forest, all vastly different landscapes yet they blend to create a masterpiece. But the most breathtaking of all: the mountains. The orange clouds shine on the sharp peaks giving them a warm glow.

Rivers of white snow are sprinkled throughout the highest points of the jagged rock. It is just how Stevey described.

"This is Cali," the woman gestures to a sign beside her. My entrancement with the view before me is broken as I look to our host. I follow her long pastel nails to the sign she is referencing. A wooden board shows the phrase *WELCOME TO CALI* in cursive gold writing. The bottom corner of the sign is broken off, erasing the remaining letters of the word for CALI. "Oh dear," the woman laughs, closing her darkened eyes. "How rude of me, I didn't even ask for your names."

"Jejune, Stevey, and Rose." As if reliving the past, Jejune's answer runs through me as I think back to how she said that when we first met Frank.

"Lovely," the woman replies. "Roses are my favorite flower." She smiles at me as I continue to massage my shoulder. "Now, before we proceed further, do you have any weapons?"

"No," Jejune states.

"Why that was an awfully quick answer." The woman looks to Jejune. "May I ask what your profession is." Jejune stares at her, remaining silent.

"Fishing," she finally replies.

"Well, I know I'm older than you young ladies, but I wasn't born yesterday." She laughs, her aged eyes crinkling her dark makeup. "Then if you're a fisher I know you have a knife on you." I glance at Jejune as Stevey looks up at her, the corner of his glasses cracked from the fall. Jejune and the woman stare at one another as Jejune slides her hand in her back pocket, revealing a knife. The woman smiles as Jejune hands it over. "Anything else?"

"No," Jejune states. The woman looks to me. I shake my head.

"Excellent. We do not allow weapons here." The woman turns back around. I look to Jejune as she gives me a quick wink. Swallowing, I release my grip on my shoulder as we continue to follow the woman. Jejune puts her arm out in front of me, stopping my motion.

"So you get to know our names but we don't get to know yours," Jejune questions, lowering her arm back down. The woman stops and turns to us all again. A soft smile forms on her boney face, a hint of confusion furrowing her thin brows.

"Why I already told you. Welcome to Cali. I am Cali."

Securing the community inside, we follow Cali through the wall of trailers. Now within the walls, my eyes scan row upon row of dimly lit tents. Unlike the small camping tents I have seen, these tents are the size of homes.

"This way," Cali smiles, leading us down a path of flickering lanterns.

Continuing with the tour, I accompany Cali down the walkway, Jejune and Stevey staying close behind. Just like the lanterns, each evenly spaced tent glows as we pass, the occasional shadow of a person going about their business shining through. Mirroring Cali's face, we stroll by people with the same dark smears under their eyes. I crane my neck around. It is as though we have stepped into a painting with the smooth sand, red mountains, and sapphire twilight sky.

"This can be yours." Cali presents a ranch style tent, the lights from within illuminating through the sheer fabric. "Consider it your new home."

"Wow!" Stevey exhales, mouth open wide as he rests on Jejune's hip.

"Please," Cali states, gesturing for us to enter. Jejune and I exchange a glance. The bloodshot in her eye glistens off the lanterns below us as I try to read her emotions. Briefly grinning to Cali, I sweep the fabric open, the weighted material unexpected as I reveal the interior of the tent.

To say the tent is magnificent would be an understatement. Replacing the sand outside, a ginormous patterned rug covers the ground. Matching the pastel color pallet, furniture throughout compliments the interior design. A comfy couch, hanging art work, wooden dining table, a full kitchen. My eyes focus on the string lights draped overhead, extending around to a corner of the tent I cannot see.

"This is better than our home JJ!" Stevey squeals. He wiggles out of Jejune's arms, skipping inside. Cali lets out a giggle as Stevey runs into the tent. He brushes past me and rounds the corner. Intrigued, I follow to see parallel bunk beds and a closed sliding door, which I can only assume is the bathroom.

"There's food in the fridge and cabinets, but if it's not to your liking, we can take a tour of the gardens tomorrow." Knocking me out of my state of amazement, I turn to Cali standing in the kitchen as Jejune remains at the tent entrance, arms crossed over her chest. "You all arrived at the perfect time. The ceremony starts when the moon rests in the center of the sky," Cali states, her hands softly moving above her head. "We'd love for you to join."

"Ceremony?" Jejune questions.

"Yes, a community gathering."

"Is it mandatory," Jejune asks.

"No," Cali responds, furrowing her brow. "But I think you'll enjoy it." She smiles, turning her attention to me as I stand in the middle of the tent.

"Thank you," I reply.

"Well, I'll let you get settled." Cali glides around the kitchen island back towards the entrance. "And I hope to see you all tonight." She gives me one last smile. Turning to face Jejune, her beaded necklaces rattle as their eyes meet. Jejune keeps her arms crossed, her scar piercing through Cali's dark concaved eyes. Silently, Cali leaves, her clothes trailing behind her. I swivel my body, taking in everything again. Jejune finally uncrosses her arms, slowly walking further into the tent.

"JJ they have sugar cookies!" Stevey announces pointing to the table.

"Don't touch that," Jejune states, rushing over to Stevey. "Still need to feel these people out." She drops her bag on the ground and the sound of metal scraping against each other echoes.

The guns.

"Look," he gleams, pulling on Jejune's arm. "A bunk bed! Do you think Charlie can sleep over?"

"Jejune," I state, following her and Stevey down the narrow path.

"Can Charlie come?" Stevey asks, looking up at Jejune, his excited eyes screaming through his broken glasses.

"Maybe," she replies, scoping out the beds and bathroom.

"Yay!" Stevey shouts, running back into the main area of the tent.

"Jejune," I press. "Our guns?"

"They don't need to know," she simply states, exploring the room as she too heads back to the main area. "Stevey come here." Kneeling down, she takes his glasses off his face.

"How are we supposed to hide them?" I plead.

"Don't worry about it," she reassures, inspecting Stevey's glasses. "I'll fix them soon okay baby."

"Okay," he replies. Jejune slides Stevey's glasses back on his face. Grabbing her bag from the ground, she heads to the kitchen. Jejune unzips her bag, placing all our food on the island counter.

"We'll eat our stuff," she instructs. "For all we know this food is poisoned."

"JJ," Stevey climbs up the tall kitchen stool. "Can I sleep on the top bunk!"

"Yes, after the ceremony," she responds, continuing to empty her bag.

"We are going to the ceremony?" I question, joining them in the kitchen. Jejune stops unloading her bag and looks directly at me.

"Oh we're going," she declares. "We need to see what this earthy crunchy freak show ceremony is all about."

V. ANGELO

It did not take long for the moon to rest in the center of the sky as Cali put. Still surprised by Jejune's willingness to attend, I go along with it; what else am I going to do. Stepping out of our luxurious tent, we easily find where the ceremony is being held. Mimicking the warm lanterns lighting our path, we make our way to a huge bonfire. Jejune reaches for Stevey's hand as we maneuver through the crowd.

Unlike the elegant chairs in the six ballroom, benches carved from trunks of trees enclose the fire. Passing by others, we find an open bench. The heat from the fire drifts towards my face as sweat layers atop my caked on makeup. I drag my moist palms on my shorts and take a look around the circle. Dark makeup is smeared under the majority of everyone's eyes, but there are a handful of people like Jejune, Stevey, and I still with spheres on their faces. Although dimly lit, I count about forty others, maybe more hidden in the shadows. Sneaking a glance to Jejune, she smirks with a raise of her eyebrows. Maybe Jejune was right. Maybe it is a freak show.

Before my mind can think about it anymore, everyone around us stands. Perplexed, I remain seated as Jejune motions for Stevey to sit on her lap. Rounding the fire, Cali appears, her attire dancing with the flame next to her. She puts her hands out and everyone proceeds to sit.

"Welcome to our ceremony. The circle of crying ceremony." Cali pauses, looking to each one of us as she walks. "This is a safe space. Share your grief, your sadness, your pain. We're here to listen and cry together." She lets her speech hang in the toasty air as she strolls towards an empty bench. "We have newcomers tonight.

We welcome you to share. Tonight, our challenge is the first." Others make sounds of approval. "The first time you shed a tear. The first time you felt suffering. The first time you let yourself be free." Cali pauses, her head falling back to look at the sky. The fire eerily flickers against her pale skin. "Avery." Cali snaps her head to a girl on the other end of the circle. "I sense your energy. Please share." Following Cali's stare, I look to Avery, her one sphere beaming off the intense moonlight.

"Um," her hands disappear under her thighs as she anxiously looks around. "It's not that great."

"It's not about greatness," Cali reassures.

"No I mean." Avery closes her eyes, continuing to nervously sit on her hands. "I mean it isn't a good story."

"But it's your story," Cali proclaims. She looks around to the others who nod in agreement. Rising from his seat, a tall man approaches Avery and sits next to her. Avery remains unmoving as the man puts his hand out for her to take. Cautiously, she places her hand in the man's palm. He smiles towards her, his darkened eyes masking his true features.

"I was twelve," Avery states, looking back out to the crowd. "My friends and I were playing in the street and a car came speeding." Avery stops. The man holding her hand nods as her glistening eyes shine off the fire. "My friend got hit and wouldn't get up." Avery quickly glues her fingers to her nose as her face becomes red. "I knew I shouldn't have been crying, but I didn't know I was. I looked to my friends and they were pointing at me and there were tears on my face." Avery wipes snot away from her nose. "After that, I never played in the street again."

"That was the first time you ever cried," Cali questions, her body hunched with emotions. Avery rapidly shakes her head as her lip quivers.

"Why did he get hit and not me," she delicately whimpers. She looks around, unable to control her crying anymore. Her gaze stops at the man holding her hand. "Why did he have to get hit at all." Bursting into tears, Avery slumps into the man as he wraps his arms around her.

"Survivors guilt," Cali shouts over her sobs. "The worst kind of guilt." Uncomfortable, I look towards Jejune as Avery's cries echo into the night. Jejune flashes her eyes at me, holding Stevey on her lap even firmer. "It is time."

Rising from her bench, Cali walks over to Avery. Everyone falls silent, Avery's faint sobs and occasional popping of firewood filling our ears. The man hugging Avery moves away, leaving her alone as her damp cheeks glow. Cali reaches her side, standing over her.

"Vanish your spheres, welcome your tears." Cali scoops her hand into the bowl and briskly brushes her fingers under Avery's eyes. The rest of the circle claps as I continue to be hypnotized by the scene unfolding. A small smile forms on Avery's face, transforming into joyful laughter as the clapping crescendos. Jejune and I remain frozen.

Abruptly, Cali turns and places her hand over her heart. Discomfort scrunches her face as she closes her eyes. Others grow concerned and stop applauding as Cali's torso begins contracting.

"Pain," Cali breathes. "Unimaginable pain." She looks up, making direct eye contact with Jejune. "Please share your story." Jejune scoffs.

"No thanks," she smirks.

"You're so guarded." Cali makes her way towards us. "Please, let it out." Cali reaches Jejune, attempting to place her hand on her arm.

"I don't need to," Jejune states, moving away from her gesture.

"We're here to listen," Cali says. The air is silent, my heartbeat pulsates in my ears, muffling the crackling fire.

"It helps," Avery adds, almost a whisper. She looks to Jejune, water still swirling in her now darkened eyes. Unfazed, Jejune remains stoic.

"If you're not ready yet, we respect that," Cali calmly replies, looking to everyone else. "But when you are, we're here to listen. Stevey?"

"He won't be sharing either," Jejune spits. Jejune continues to stare at Cali, her scar redder than the fire.

"Very well." Cali turns to me. "Rose?"

"Oh, not tonight." *Please move on.*

"I'll share Cali," an older woman says, dark makeup already smeared under her eyes. Smiling, Cali thanks her with a nod.

As the older woman begins her tale, Cali crosses the light from the fire. I see her tightly clutching the bowl in her hand, the whites of her knuckles spreading like cream being poured in a cup of coffee. With my heartbeat still predominant, I once again look to Jejune. The bloodshot in her eye fixates on me, her jaw clenched with a hint of anger.

I may not know much about Cali, but I am certain this is the mysterious piece of land I saw. It has to be.

'Vanish your spheres, welcome your tears.'

With a motto such as that, of course Amella would want to keep this place a secret. This place is nothing like Amella, it is the furthest thing. Jejune was right, this is a freak show.

The ceremony went on for another hour. Others shared stories of their first. There were tears. There was applause. There was Cali ready to vanish more spheres. Heading back to the tent for the night, I really do not know what to think of it all.

"That was… interesting," I say, closing the opening to our tent.

"A little too culty for my liking," Jejune laughs.

"What's culty mean?" Stevey asks.

"Nothing you gotta worry about," Jejune smirks, ruffling his thin hair. Stevey giggles as Jejune makes her way into the kitchen, opening a can of the food we brought. "Come here and eat before bed."

"Can I have –" Stevey begins to ask, pointing to the sugar cookies.

"No," Jejune snaps. "Eat this." Obeying, Stevey hops up onto the stool as Jejune hands him a spoon from her bag. Just like when we arrived, I inspect the interior decor, my eyes observing the elegance all around. "You want any Rose?" I look to Jejune, her hand extending an open bag of chips. I shake my head, walking into the main room. Puzzled, I examine the furnishments closer. Spotless. How is furniture in a sandy desert spotless?

"All done!" Stevey shouts, pushing his empty can away from him.

"Good job," Jejune smiles, kissing him on the forehead. "Bed time little man." Stevey jumps off the stool as Jejune grabs her bag, riffling for his pajamas. Stevey takes his clothes and runs down the hall, using all his strength to slide the bathroom door shut. "What a day," Jejune states, shoveling more chips in her mouth.

"Yeah," I say, turning back to the furniture. "How do you think –" Jejune suddenly hunches over, clamping her hand on her chest.

"Pain, unimaginable pain," Jejune dramatically cries, imitating Cali earlier. "What an actress," she scoffs, slamming her elbows on the kitchen counter continuing to munch on chips.

"How do you think they keep the tents so clean?" Jejune does not answer, the chewing of her chips echoing. "Where did they get this furniture anyway?" Jejune places the chip bag down, examining the tent just as I am.

"Hmm," she frowns. "That's a good question." I nod, taking more notice of everything in this tent. I stop, looking back to Jejune.

"That ceremony was –"

"Weird," she replies, taking the words out of my mouth.

"Yeah." Glad it was not just me who thought that.

"And the black makeup. Nah, never wearing that shit." A gasp grabs our attention as Stevey is standing in the room, hands over his ears. "Sorry."

"I felt bad for that one girl who lost her friend," Stevey softly says, uncovering his ears.

"I know baby," Jejune smiles, walking over to him. "Ready for bed?"

"Top bunk," he begs, body bouncing as he anxiously clenches his pajamas.

"Well," Jejune states, Stevey's smile diminishing. "Okay I guess," she smirks, his face lighting back up.

"Yay!" he shouts, running down the hallway.

"Coming to bed?" Jejune asks me.

"Going to eat something then I will." Jejune nods, following Stevey down the hallway.

Entering the kitchen, I open the cabinets before me. Dishes, cups, snacks. I make my way to the fridge as Jejune and Stevey's conversation faintly fills my ears. Water, eggs, cheese. I close the fridge, turning back to our food on the island counter. Although we had a long day of traveling, I do not have much of an appetite. I take a seat and pick up the chip bag, slowly filling my stomach with some sustenance.

Now sitting, the weight of today smacks me like a wave. It feels so long ago, but this morning I was in the West playing the role of Aster. I wonder how she is doing. I wish there was a way to tell her that we found this place. That this place *does* exist. I gnaw on more chips as my mind replays the recent events. Cali. So this mysterious piece of land is Cali. My memory flashes to Cali's hand at the ceremony, tensely gripping the bowl full of dark makeup. The way she held that bowl seemed angry. Was she upset we did not participate? I thought after all this time I would find some relief discovering this place, finally solving the mysterious piece of land, but I am just more confused. It is only the first night though. Tomorrow is a new day. It will be interesting to see how Cali operates during the daytime.

After yesterday my body was completely exhausted. I woke up in the same position I fell asleep in; I truly slept like a rock. Just like the kitchen cabinets, the bathroom is stocked with fresh towels, soap, toothbrushes, and a few other toiletries. It is as if the tent was prepared for our arrival. I took extra time to scrub my face, making sure my makeup and Aster's freckles were removed. Staring at my reflection this morning, I look more like myself.

Over the huge bags under my eyes, my five spheres pop all the more with my blonde hair. A sudden feeling of guilt passes through me. Today is Counting Day. My parents must be worried. Pressure forms at the bridge of my nose. I have to contact them. I hope there is a phone I can use around here. Taking a deep breath, I gather myself and head into the main room.

"She's back," Jejune jokes. It takes me a second but then I realize she means my five spheres. Oddly, Jejune is wearing the same clothes as yesterday, her hat is backwards, and there are still spots of dirt on her from our fall.

"Did you sleep at all?"

"Of course not," she laughs, closing the fridge. "Gotta stay alert." Jejune stops in the middle of the kitchen holding up a finger. "Do you hear that?" I listen, trying to hear what she is referring to.

"No?" I question, joining Stevey on the couch.

"Exactly," she exclaims. "It's very quiet. Too quiet."

"Good morning!" Cali shouts outside the tent, breaking the silence. "I don't want to intrude but may I come in?"

"For someone who doesn't want to intrude you're intruding," Jejune mumbles. I snap my head to Jejune, awkwardly waiting on what to do.

"Sure," I shout back. Irritated, Jejune rolls her eyes at me. I shrug, attempting to defend myself.

"Good morn –" Cali freezes as she enters the tent. "Rose your face."

My face? What is wrong with my face?

"Oh," I smile. "I was wearing makeup."

"Makeup?" Cali tilts her head, her crown of flowers shifting. Subtly, her eyes change. Like the burst of a lightning strike; brisk but brightly noticeable. She exhales, gently shaking her head. "We're all having breakfast," she continues, "but I see you may have already eaten," gesturing to the empty cans in the kitchen.

"Yup," Jejune replies, throwing away the cans from the night before.

"Well we have fruit, pancakes, waffles, and –"

"Waffles?" Stevey asks.

"Yes," Cali smiles, turning her attention to Stevey. "With your own toppings, most of the kids love it."

"Kids?" Stevey leaps off the couch running to the kitchen. "JJ, you think Charlie is there?"

"Stevey –" Jejune starts to say.

"Why doesn't he come," Cali interrupts. Jejune stops cleaning and looks to Cali. "He can meet some kids his age." Cali remains smiling, her doe eyes unblinking at Jejune.

"Please JJ," Stevey bounces, biting his lower lip. Jejune puts down the plate she is holding and approaches him.

"I can take him." Cali extends her arm draped in fabric towards Stevey. Jejune snaps her head up, her scar piercing Cali's dark eyes. She grabs Stevey's hand and steps in front of him, forcing Cali to look at her.

"Lead the way," Jejune firmly replies. Cali retracts her arm, her wavy hair swaying as she pivots around. Annoyed, Jejune glares at me as she faces her hat front before walking out into the morning sun. I slowly rise off the couch and follow.

Similar to last night, we walk down the path of now unlit lanterns towards the breakfast area. Turning my head, I am able to see the benches surrounding the ceremony more clearly with the sunlight. The craftsmanship is beautiful. Each piece is smoothly sanded to perfection, a thin glossy coat of protection making the benches look brand new. As we continue, the calm murmurs in the breakfast area capture my attention. Not as fancy as the ceremony benches, unstained wood provide picnic style seating for everyone. Cali stops at the buffet, neatly organized with a plethora of food options.

"Please don't be shy," Cali states, handing us bamboo plates. "There are no weighing stations here."

"See you like wood," Jejune comments, grabbing a matching set of utensils.

"We make our kitchenware by hand. Everything here is made by us," Cali smiles. "Self sustaining in every aspect. You'll see during the tour." Cali's smile is frozen on her face as she looks to Jejune and Stevey, ignoring my presence. "But please," she shouts, scaring me a little. "Eat first."

Cautious of ruining the elegant display, my stomach growls at the food before us. I guess I am hungrier than I thought. Unlike me, Jejune digs in, creating a pile of breakfast assortments. I laugh as she holds a peach midair.

"What?" she questions.

"I thought you said the food was poisoned."

"No one back there has dropped dead yet," she states, referring to the others dining behind us. "So I guess we're fine." Joining Jejune, I too stack my plate with a pyramid of food. After Jejune helps Stevey with his selection, we turn around looking for an open picnic bench. "Time to mingle," she exhales, making her way to the emptiest table we can find. "Do you mind," Jejune stands, asking the table.

"Of course not," an older woman states. "Please join us." We all scoot our way in, immediately digging into our food. "Jejune, Rose, Stevey," the woman says, mixing up my name with Jejune's.

"Close," Jejune smirks, shoveling a forkful of food in her mouth.

"Sorry, my memory is not so great. Roses are a beautiful flower," she smiles. "I haven't seen one in decades, but they would be lovely in our centerpieces." She looks to the wooden cube holding an arrangement of delicate flowers. "I'm Wila." She places her hand gently on the person next to her. "This is Forest." The man eats his food, his dark eyes looking down at his plate. "Did you enjoy the ceremony?" I continue chewing, hoping Jejune will take this one.

"Definitely an experience," Jejune states, raising her eyebrows.

"It truly is," she replies, obviously missing Jejune's sarcasm. "Forest shared last week, such a wonderful story he told." Forest nods as his darkened eyes flicker to our faces, continuing to peck at his food.

"Sorry we had to miss it," Jejune mockingly replies.

"It'll be nice to hear your stories next week."

"Well, in order for that –"

"The ceremony is every week?" I ask, cutting off yet another sarcastic Jejune response.

"Yes," Wila breathes joyfully. "I wish it was nightly." I glance at Jejune, a smirk forming on her face, gearing up for another reply.

"I hope your first breakfast here is to your liking," Cali gleams, hovering above our table just in time before Jejune continued. "Stevey, why don't you join the other kids." She extends her arms forward to a circular table full of children.

"Can I?" Stevey asks, whipping his head up at Jejune.

"Yeah, but come back when you're done," she states. Jejune reaches to brush his hair but he runs away before she can.

"He seems so sweet," Wila states. I smile back as Jejune's neck remains craned, following Stevey's path. "My granddaughter Ivy is over there."

"You have a granddaughter here?" I question, trying to softly crunch on a piece of toast.

"Born and raised, like my son," she turns, rubbing Forest on the back.

"How long have you been here?"

"Oh my," Wila chuckles. "For as long as I can remember." She looks up at Cali, their aged eyes mirroring one another. I nod, looking to Jejune, who finally has come back to the conversation.

"I don't want to rush you," Cali says, turning her attention to Jejune and I. "But when you're finished with your meal, we can start the tour."

"Sounds good boss," Jejune states, raising her wooden cup to her. Cali laughs, immediately stopping as she walks away.

"The tour is so much fun," Wila cheers, leaning over the table. "So much to explore and so many roles to choose from."

"Hmm?" Jejune mumbles, removing the cup from her lips.

"Your roles." Wila gasps. "Oh Forest, I ruined it." She buries her head in her hands as Forest silently continues his meal.

"Ruined what exactly?" Jejune asks, unfazed by Wila's dramatic reaction, sneaking a glance to check on Stevey. Calming herself down, Wila strokes the topaz flowers around her neck.

"Your roles," she repeats. "You'll get to choose what you do for Cali." Not responding, Jejune and I look to one another, equally confused.

"So, like a job?" I question, trying to understand.

"Oh no," Wila whispers. "Cali does *not* like the term job."

"But it's a job," Jejune states, nodding towards Wila.

"No, it is a role," she implores. "It is a role for Cali."

"Cali the place or Cali the person," Jejune smirks.

"Cali the place." Wila grips her necklace, halting her gentleness. She stares at us, her charcoal makeup growing darker as her face becomes intensely serious. "You're both a part of Cali now. You have to do your part."

Tense silence washes over our table. Uneasy, I focus on my cloth napkin, holding it down as a gust of wind blows. I continue to avoid Wila's eye contact as Jejune loudly clears her throat, bringing her cup back to her lips.

"Well," Wila releases her firm hold on her necklace. "Enjoy the tour. I can't wait to hear about it at breakfast tomorrow." She smiles as she grabs her plate and stands. Firmly rubbing Forest's back, he wipes his napkin over his stubble beard and follows.

"Alrighty," Jejune comments, peering into her cup. "Maybe I shouldn't drink this. Something in the water, no one can take a joke." Still uncomfortable, I fidget with the remaining food on my plate. "She's a damn whack job if she thinks we're gonna sit with her tomorrow." Jejune and I share a laugh as I take one final bite of my toast.

With Wila gone, I stare at the view in front of us. Past the ceremony area the tops of the mountains hover with a morning lavender tint. We made it. We are *actually* here. The longer I stare at the mountains, the more I think about what I should be doing today. I should be by my mom and dad's side in Amella uniform. Gazing out the clear windows of the train, taking in the beauty of North Amella. Sensing eyes on me, my head turns to see Jejune staring at me. I stare back, the bloodshot in her eye flickering like an image in a flipbook.

"Still getting used to the new look."

"Me too," I confess. "I used way too much shampoo this morning."

"I know that feeling," she jokes. We both heave over with laughter. Jejune looks behind her and stops laughing. Concerned, I follow her eyesight to see the children at the kid's table surrounding Stevey and pointing at him.

"Wait," I beg as Jejune unwedges from the table. Exhaling, I accompany her as she sprints towards Stevey. The last thing I need is for Jejune to go off on a bunch of children and make a scene. I squint as her thick boots kick up sand with each stride. Speeding up, I catch up as she skids to a halt.

"Your glasses are broken," a girl says, pointing at Stevey's face.

"I know," Stevey slumps his head.

"Put your –" Jejune starts.

"Can I try them on?" the girl gleams, cutting Jejune off. Lowering her pointed finger, the girl steps closer to Stevey.

"You like them?" Stevey asks, bringing his head up.

"They're cool."

"I want to try them on next!" another boy shouts. Beaming, Stevey rips his glasses off and hands them to the girl. She hastily puts them on and turns to show the others who grab at her to try on next.

"Stevey, you okay?" Jejune questions, squatting next to him.

"Yeah. Why?" his tiny voice asks confused.

"Just," Jejune looks to the swarm of kids lining up to try on his glasses. "Your glasses. You're okay with them taking them?"

"They aren't taking them," Stevey giggles. "They're my friends." A smile spreads across his petite face as he looks at Jejune, their green eyes reflecting. "They said I am cool JJ."

"Glasses," Cali states behind us. "Stevey did you know you're the only one in Cali to wear glasses." Stevey's mouth opens with shock. "That's pretty special."

21

Stevey turns his head back to Jejune with pure happiness.

"You're one of a kind little man," Jejune smirks, scratching his head.

"As much as I'm interrupting today, I do want to start the tour." Before we can respond, Cali turns to the other kids. "Children, return Stevey's glasses." The kids stop laughing and hand him his glasses. "What do we say?"

"Thank you," the kids reply in harmony with their identical dark eyes. The girl who called Stevey's glasses cool quickly waves before running with the others. Cali turns her attention back to the three of us as Stevey places his glasses back on.

"It's so wonderful you're making friends Stevey," she comments. He smiles as Jejune faces her back to Stevey to jump on. He flings onto her and giggles as she hoists him up. "Let's get started, shall we?"

Obeying commands, we begin the tour. Adjacent to our living quarters, we reach a wide field of open tents bustling with various work stations. As we walk, Cali describes each station's purpose. I vaguely listen as I focus on the organized chaos engulfing my senses. The clothing station's shelves are stuffed full with a rainbow of swatches. Pounding sewing machines compete against one another as workers carefully drag fabric through.

"Feel free to come by anytime you want to update your wardrobe," Cali smirks. My eyes and ears focus on the next station as the incessant sewing machines fade away. Tables of dense burlap bags overflow with countless ingredients. Grains, seeds, flour. Bag upon bag upon bag.

Continuing on, we pass more lively stations. An outdoor garden with rich soil sprouting multiple plants, vegetables, and fruits. A woodworking station cutting, sanding, and gluing any and everything. A greenhouse station, which I was happy we walked past and did not go inside considering I could taste the thickness of the humidity. And finally, one station that Stevey particularly enjoys.

"Chocolate!" he cheers. Jejune crouches down for Stevey to dismount.

"Not quite," Cali confesses, approaching the short trees. "Cacao."

"Cacao?" he repeats.

"The seeds that make chocolate." Intrigued, we watch Cali approach a tree littered with what look to be wrinkled footballs. "River!" Following Cali's gaze, a young man approaches us. "Could you?" she asks, stepping away. Nodding, River uses a curved knife to disconnect the seed from the tree, firmly catching it in his hand. Effortlessly, he drags the knife over the seed, perfectly splitting it in half.

"They're really sweet," River states, bending down to show Stevey the sticky inside. "Try one," he encourages.

"That doesn't look like chocolate," Stevey remarks, his small eyebrows crinkling. Similar to Stevey, I eyeball the contents. Gooey, bright white sardined beans rest on the inside. Unmoving, Stevey continues to stare.

"Little man here isn't a fan of slimy surfaces," Jejune chuckles, pinching one free with her fingers. She bites into the seed, placing the other half in Stevey's mouth. River swivels the seeds towards me, I too pinching a seed from the mushy inside. Hesitant, I inspect the seed before joining Jejune and Stevey in this taste test. It does not taste like chocolate, but it is still very sweet. Stevey chews largely, River and Cali laughing at his munching.

"If you don't like it, you can spit it out baby," Jejune reassures.

"I like it. This makes chocolate?" he asks, tilting his head to River.

"It does," he grins, popping a seed in his mouth. "You can join me sometime and we can make a bar together." A smile grows across Stevey's face.

"Thank you River," Cali says as he walks away, popping another seed in his mouth. "Don't eat too much more," she exhales. "As you can see, we only have a handful of these trees, so chocolate is a limited treat around here. But now, my favorite." Cali swoops past the cacao trees, her eyes wide with anticipation. Anxious to see where we are going, we quickly follow to be met with a field of greenery.

"Corn," Cali exclaims joyfully. "This is one of our most important crops we grow." The strong stems barely bend in the morning wind as slits of the rising sun cut through the leaves.

"Corn?" Jejune questions.

"Why yes," Cali states. "If corn dies, humans die."

"Cheerful," Jejune smirks. I scan the rows of plants, spreading long past where my vision can see. Nothing but corn.

"What is the other crop?" I ask. Cali tilts her head. "You said corn is one of the most important crops. What is the other?"

"Oh dear. I seemed to have misspoken. This is our most important crop," sweeping her draped arm towards the corn. "But our most important station, I should've said, is something else."

"And that would be…" Jejune trails off.

"Look!" Stevey shouts, sending our attention across the way.

Unlike the other hustling stations, this station is moving in slow motion. The honey station. Low hums of buzzing bees circulate through the air as workers carefully slide honeycomb panels in and out. I watch the insects bounce from the worker's thick gloves to the thin netting protecting their face.

"Are there other animals?" Stevey squeals, running towards the station.

"No animals here," Cali sharply replies as we all join Stevey. "Just bees. We don't like the children to get attached."

"So where do you get your meat?" Jejune inquires.

"Meat is shipped here." I revert my focus from the bees to Cali. I quietly clear the nerves in my throat, unsure if I should ask this question.

"Is there a phone I can use?"

"Phone?" Cali asks as if this is the first time she has heard the word.

"Yes, a phone." If supplies are shipped then Cali must have a line of communication.

"Why will you be needing a phone?"

"I would like to make a call." I wait as Cali hesitates to respond.

"Sorry," she smiles. "There are no phones here." The warm breeze soothes the numbness washing over my body. My heart sinks. No phone. How will I communicate with my mom and dad? How will I be able to let them know where I am? The vibrating bees deafen my thoughts, forcing my ears to rejoin the conversation. "Stevey will have the opportunity to bee keep with his friends at school."

"I can!" Stevey shouts.

"What will he be learning?" Jejune questions. "Is there a curriculum?"

"There is a curriculum," Cali smiles. Jejune nods, circling around.

"Where's the school?"

"Why, Cali is our school," she sings, spreading her arms out. Jejune crosses her strong, tanned arms over her chest.

"So, no classroom?"

"Cali is the classroom." Jejune exhales.

"A real answer Cali, no metaphors." Gathering her thoughts, Cali's smile washes away.

"Specific curriculum I don't know," she confesses. "His teacher could provide you with more insight. I'll be sure to arrange a meeting for you." Jejune nods. "Let's continue onto the other important station. I should mention," she pauses, turning to face all of us. "This next part of the tour will take a couple of hours, are you all okay with that?" A couple of hours? How big is this place?

"We got nothing better to do," Jejune shrugs.

"Splendid!" Cali cheers. "We'll first stop by the breakfast area to get some water for our travels, it is a considerable hike."

"Hike," Jejune scoffs. "We going up the mountain or something."

"Yes actually." We all look to Cali as she stares back at us. "Are you still okay with that."

"Can we go JJ?" Stevey pleads. "I want to climb a mountain." Jejune looks down at Stevey, ruffling his wavy hair.

"Sure baby," she smiles.

"Rose I want you to come." Stevey skips over to me, reaching for my hand. "Will you come too?" My heart melts as his tiny fingers interlock with mine. I think back to us on the boat when he told me how cool it would be to climb a mountain. I have never climbed a mountain either. I smile like the little kid Stevey is.

"We got nothing better to do," I say, repeating Jejune's words. Stevey lets go of my hand, jumping for joy. Jejune mouths a thank you to me as I smile in return. Cali giggles, heading to the breakfast area as Jejune hoists Stevey on her back.

"Mountains, mountains, mountains," Stevey sings as he hugs Jejune's shoulders. Trailing behind the three of them, my smile fades as I take one last look at the beekeepers, their hands meticulously dancing with the singing bugs. The air pulsates with their buzzing like that of a busy dial on a phone. I have to find a phone. I need to find a phone.

V. ANGELO

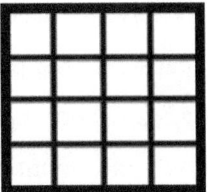

The amber sand morphs into hard pebbles the further we hike. As we trudge to the next station, we take a break with Cali's tree workers. While trees are being chopped for wood, we gulp down water as we prepare for the steep incline up ahead. Never climbing a mountain before, I did not expect the lower portion to be surrounded by immense color. Blossoming flowers, towering cacti, wild berries sprouting by our feet. The change from sand to greenery is so drastic. Almost unnatural.

"Apologies," Cali breathes. "My knees aren't as limber as when I was young." She inhales, winded in her speech. "We'll have to see the station from here." We all nod. Cali bows her head, still breathing deeply. After a few more heavy steps, we approach a flattened piece of ground. The landing resembles a high rise balcony tightly enclosed with purple perennials.

"Please note, the station is a no access area," Cali stresses. "So we'll only be able to see the station from afar."

"Secretive, are we?" Jejune remarks, stepping up to the landing still with Stevey dangling on her back.

"No secrets. It's for everyone's safety." Joining them, I too step up onto the mountain's balcony. Arms clasped in front to keep her attire from blowing about, Cali looks out across the sky. "These are our solar panels." Jejune, Stevey, and I turn our heads, searching for what she is referring to. Beyond the work stations, beyond the living quarters, and far beyond the trailer walls, a sea of solar panels drown out the acres of sand.

"Cool!" Stevey stares in awe. He scoots down Jejune's back and runs to the edge. Rising to his tippy toes, he leans over the perennials.

"Concentrated solar panels," Cali continues. "The heat that radiates off them is extremely hot." My eyes scan each one, counting a few dozen. "The temperature the panels reach could evaporate a bird flying over. Very high heat, not safe for us."

"That makes electricity," Stevey points, staggering to keep his balance.

"Precisely," Cali smiles, looking down at him. "Very smart Stevey. Due to the high temperatures, we keep our distance."

"You've had no issues?" Jejune questions, scanning over the monstruous reflective squares. Cali shakes her head. "They power all of Cali?"

"Impressive right," she remarks. "We're in the perfect spot for maximum amount of sun." Curious, I join in the conversation by asking my own question.

"What if there is an issue?" I look back to Cali, waiting for an answer.

"There are none." Her dark eyes slant slightly. I stay silent, Cali's strict tone making me stop.

"What if someone needs to go out and fix one?" Jejune continues. "They couldn't possibly be perfect all the time."

"The gentleman who installed these was a genius." Cali smiles and turns her head, admiring the panels. "They can resist anything."

"What about rain?" Jejune asks.

"It never rains in Cali."

"It does not rain?" I ask.

"No," Cali replies, still overlooking the view.

"Never?" Cali slowly turns her head towards me, gently moving a piece of tangerine hair off her face.

"Never." Uncomfortable, I flick my eyes to the panels. "As I've previously stated, Cali is in the perfect spot to utilize the sun's full potential." She claps, the sound vibrating loudly in the open air. "That concludes our tour."

"Nah wait," Jejune scoffs. "You're telling me that those," Jejune nods her head to the farm of panels. "Power *everything* in Cali."

"Why is that so hard to believe," Cali calmy asks.

"Not hard to believe," Jejune frowns. "I think it's just," she ponders, securing her hands to her hips. "Risky to have only one energy source. Is it not?" Cali does not answer. Swallowing, my heartbeat increases. If there is one thing Jejune can be, it is pushy. I get the sense Cali does not like pushy.

"I would have to politely disagree with you Jejune. Seeing as we have had no issues, it's not risky at all." Jejune nods, accepting Cali's response. "Let's move on." Her dark eye makeup creases with a forced smile. "And discuss you two."

"Our roles," Jejune states, hitching her eyebrows up. Cali's smile disappears as an aura of intensity consumes her aged face.

"You know about your roles?" Cali questions. Jejune clenches her teeth.

"Oh, about that," Jejune replies. "Wila kinda spilled the beans."

"She did?" Cali closes her eyes. "Please forgive Wila for ruining the surprise." A frown twitches across her face as she tries to maintain her smile, fluttering her eyes open. My bones tighten as I continue to watch Cali control her emotions. "Rose I'm deeply sorry. There is no Film Industry."

"No need to apologize," I reassure with a quick nod.

"Pity a top sphere holder such as yourself will not be rewarded for your work." I cease my nodding as Cali's face shifts. "I know we'll find a role that will fulfill you." I stare into her dark eyes, watching the miniscule movement of her large pupils. Her eyes jump to each sphere like the second hand ticking on a clock. As if time is standing still, my face sinks as a wave of realization strikes me. Cali snaps

29

her focus away, breaking our trance.

"Jejune, we do in fact have fishing," she happily cheers.

"Oh," Jejune utters. "You don't ship them here?"

"Why would we ship them?"

"You said earlier you ship all your meat." Swinging her hands, Cali covers her mouth and begins laughing.

"I did, didn't I," she admits, her words muffled through her cupped hands. I turn to Jejune as Cali's chortle continues to fill our ears. Composing herself, we face her again. "Fish we catch here in the river."

"But fish are meat," Jejune states, her brow furrowing.

"Yes, but," Cali looks to the sky, gathering her words. "Fish aren't prepared in such a barbaric way to scar the children. They can't get attached as they would other animals."

"Wow," Jejune yells, banging her head forward. Stevey turns around as we all look to Jejune, caught off guard by her shout. "So you're saying my attachment to my first fish Goldy the goldfish means nothing in your eyes." I scoff and shake my head, Stevey giggling slightly.

"Oh, you're joking," Cali questions, looking to Stevey and I for reassurance. Stevey continues to giggle as I nod slightly. "That went right over my head," she admits. "Anyways, Jejune, I'll arrange a meeting for you and Stevey's teacher."

"Much appreciated," Jejune responds, tipping her hat.

"You're more than welcome to continue hiking the mountain." Cali swivels her body, craning her neck up. "Just follow the trail."

"Can we! Can we!" Stevey asks, running to Jejune's side.

"I don't know," Jejune says, straining her neck to look up. "Rose?"

"Oh no, you two go," I reply. "Got to get back before –"

"You were going to say curfew, weren't you?" Cali interrupts. A large grin spreads across her face. "You don't have to worry about that here."

"No curfew!" Stevey looks to all of us as Cali and I continue to stare at one another. "We can stay here all night!"

"Stevey," Jejune exhales. "I know you're excited but –"

"If not today another day," Cali shouts, breaking eye contact with me. "The mountains are always here Stevey." She smiles at him as his face sinks.

"Fine," he mumbles, stomping his tiny foot.

"Explore as long as you would like." Cali slowly makes her way down the mountain. I watch as her lengthy hair swings left to right, the flowers throughout her hair bouncing with each step down. Similar to last night's ceremony, I catch a glimpse of Cali's hand through her draped shawl, clenched tight. Veins protruding out. Knuckles turning white. I vaguely hear my name and snap out of my trance.

"What?" I question, blinking towards Jejune.

"We'll come back tomorrow, right." Jejune raises her eyebrows at me.

"Right," I quickly smile, looking towards Stevey. "Tomorrow."

"Yay!" Stevey takes Jejune's hand as they walk the inclined ground.

"Be careful baby," Jejune states, safely guiding him down the trail. Before joining, I take one last look over Cali's dry land spreading for miles.

Hopping off the landing, I scoot inch by inch down the slope, attempting not to fall. Making it back on flat ground, we head towards the living quarters to reside for the evening. As the sun sets and the lanterns below us start to glow, I replay all the areas we toured. Work stations. Gardens. Greenhouse. Crops. Mountains. Solar panels. Then my recounting stops. Wait. Cali mentioned there is no Film Industry here. My mind swells with anxiety. How does Cali know I work in the Film Industry? I never told Cali I work in the Film Industry.

31

"Man, I'm tired," Jejune states, jumping onto the couch. Stevey leaps on top of her as she lets out a painful grunt, pretending he crushed her. Equally as exhausted, I sit on one of the kitchen stools, rummaging through the food on the counter. "Rose." I look to Jejune, who has her hands up. I reach across the table for a bag of chips and hurl them across the room.

"JJ," Stevey squeals. "Can I *please* have a sugar cookie now." I follow Stevey's small finger pointing to the basket on the wooden table. Stevey anxiously waits as Jejune munches on her chip. Dragging it out, she keeps chewing. "JJ!" She dramatically swallows, a small laugh escaping my mouth.

"That was a big chip," she jokes, smiling at Stevey. "You can have one. Get me one too," she adds as he rushes to the table.

"Rose, do you want one?" Stevey innocently asks me.

"Sure," I smile. Stevey brings a cookie over to me and jumps right back on the couch, snuggling up to Jejune. Silently, we enjoy our sugar cookies. After consuming mine I am craving another one, my body needing to be replenished after all of today's walking.

"Go change baby," Jejune states, rubbing his wild blonde hair. With much effort, Stevey closes the bathroom door, leaving Jejune and I alone.

Groaning, Jejune gets off the couch and makes her way to the kitchen. Joining me, she grabs the pile of snacks on the table and starts organizing them. I listen, making sure Stevey is still in the bathroom, not within earshot.

"How do you feel about Cali?" I ask.

"Cali the place or Cali the person," Jejune smirks, continuing to move snack bags around. I smile but then proceed with my thoughts.

"I have a feeling she does not like me," I confess.

"What's not to like?"

"She is always staring at my spheres. Does she stare at yours?"

"Don't know and don't care. The beauty of a hat." I nod, watching Jejune rearrange the snacks. She was definitely looking at my spheres. No not looking, counting. I saw her eyes dart to each one. Even how she reacted to seeing my face. My regular face. She was so taken aback that I was wearing makeup, as if I was hiding my true identity from her. And that pity statement? I do not need pity for not having a Film Industry role here. I hope she –

"Yo, you good?" Jejune tosses a snack bag in my direction, knocking me back to the dimly lit tent.

"Yeah, just wish I could find a phone."

"I'm sure Elle and Henry are fine," Jejune laughs. "And by fine, I mean your mom pacing nonstop in her robe and your dad repeating everything will be okay. She's probably got one hidden. Miss we-get-our-meat-shipped, so she's gotta communicate with someone somehow." Before I can respond, my ears fill with Stevey's faint footsteps running down the hall.

"I brushed my teeth and changed into my pjs," he proudly declares.

"You didn't even need my help." Jejune drops the snacks in her hand and approaches Stevey. "Good job little man. Bed time." Leaving me alone with my thoughts, they both head down the hallway.

As I sit, the aches in my muscles throb, sending pinches of discomfort through my legs, arms, and shoulders as I reminisce on all the running, running, and running. Running from the crew members. Running from the sirens. Crashing down into this place. Rowing. Killing. Shooting. Haircut. Acting. Bullet. Phone. Phone. I need a phone. All at once the journey I have been on floods my brain and soon my eyes. Shakily, I connect my fingers to my cheeks. I bring my hands back, allowing my hazy eyes to readjust. Now in focus, I see my fingertips are soaked with water.

Quietly, I tug my shirt up to my eyes, my tears absorbing into the fabric on my neckline. Not wanting to grab the attention of Jejune or Stevey, I freeze in this position as I let more tears roll off my eyelids. Crying used to be an unknown feeling for me, but now, it is such a release. I shut my eyes, squeezing out the remaining water inside like a heavily filled sponge. I shout in my mind to calm down, but I can't. Right now, the negative voice is winning, and it is much louder than the positive one. Breathing deeply, I open my eyes. It hits me how much I am dreading the morning. Once morning comes, I will have a new face to look at. Once morning comes, everyone will have a new face to look at. More importantly, Cali will see I am no longer a five. She will only have four spheres to study, judge, and criticize.

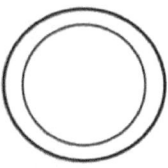

Thank you to the universe. Luckily, Cali arranged Jejune's meeting with Stevey's teacher first thing this morning. As they ate breakfast and got ready, I stayed under the sheets, shielding my face, buying myself more time before I have to show the new me. After confirming I was totally alone, I crawled my way out of bed and into the bathroom.

Avoiding my reflection for as long as possible, I immediately shower. I eventually swallowed my pride and faced the mirror. Three days. In three days I have gone from a six to a four. Just as Cali did, my eyes count each sphere on my face. I cannot cry another day. If I make this a routine, I will have no spheres in a few days. I have to be stronger than this.

With no television, I occupy my mind by tidying around the tent. Enjoying some alone time, I silently unpack and organize my clothes. Seems as though we will be staying here for a while, so might as well get comfortable. I hope I am not penalized too harshly for not returning to work. There are no vein scanners here I can use to add extra vacation days to my leave.

After unpacking my bags, I decide to move Jejune's stuff into the hallway. Walking down the narrow path, I swing her bag around and stop. Swinging again, I bring my ear to Jejune's bag. Nothing. No sound of clinking metal. Panicked, I unzip and drop the bag to the floor, furiously feeling for the guns, but my hands feel nothing. The bag is empty.

"I'm back!" As Jejune's voice echoes towards me, I stop searching. "Change of plans, Stevey joined the other kids for school today after meeting the teacher. Didn't want me around, he really is growing up." I remain frozen, hoping she does not hear me. "Rose?"

"Yeah, just unpacking," I blurt out as I hear her walking my way. I pinch the zipper on her bag, gliding the metal with the speed of an inch worm.

"So turns out," she continues, redirecting herself to the kitchen. "Not only is there communal breakfast, but dinner as well. Stevey wants to eat at the kid's table which means I gotta go. If you come with me, then I won't be stuck with that crazy Wila lady." Almost there, I finish closing her bag, slowly rising back to a standing position. "Rose, you alright?"

Not wanting to drag it out, I place her bag on the ground and make my grand entrance. Emerging from the dark hallway, I shamefully reveal myself. As Jejune closes the fridge our eyes meet.

"Oh," she states with an eyebrow raise. "You wanna talk about it?" I flutter my eyes down and shake my head. "Guess I'm the top sphere holder now," she chuckles, attempting to lighten the mood. Joining her in the kitchen, Jejune shushes the silence as she cleans the dishes in the sink. Turning my head back to the hallway, I make myself heard over the running water.

"Where are the guns?"

"I hid them." I look back to Jejune as she washes dishes.

"How do you know how to shoot a gun."

"Does it matter," she exhales. I know I have asked this question multiple times and this topic with her may not end well, but I need answers.

"Amella citizens do not have guns," I say, reciting Amella law.

"Your point."

"You," I stop. "We," correcting myself, "are Amella citizens."

"Looks like we're part of the Cali clan now." Our conversation stops as Jejune scrubs a plate. With as much courage as I can find in my vulnerable body, I ask my next question, hoping Jejune's response shows I am not alone.

"Do you think about them?" Jejune does not answer. "The two night crew you killed," I barely stammer out. Still silence. "I think about them –"

"You think I don't Rose," Jejune snaps, finally turning her head towards me. The sink continues to run as we stare at one another.

"You don't seem –"

"Don't seem what?" Jejune's scar pierces me as I contemplate if I should say what is on my mind. My throat opens up, uttering the word.

"Remorseful." Jejune scoffs.

"Sorry I'm not reacting the way you'd like." She faces forward, resuming her cleaning of dishes. "But I have Stevey to think about. I can't mope around all day and relive the decision I made. I made it, it's done, move on."

"How can you just move –"

"Because I have to." Aggravated, Jejune shoves the faucet off. Her neck dangles as she shakes her head. Suddenly, she bangs on the counter, making me jump. "It was my hand that connected with their neck and took their life. It was my finger that pulled the trigger so a bullet wouldn't hit you or Stevey." Anger swirls in Jejune's eyes. "I protected us."

"You didn't have to do it Jejune," I state. "We could have talked –"

"I had to," she sneers, the bloodshot in her eye pulsating. I study Jejune's face, comprehending the hatred emanating off her.

"Had to or wanted to?" I rebuttal. Blinking, the hatred in her face fades. Fast footsteps grab Jejune and I's attention, interrupting our heated discussion.

"JJ!" Stevey shouts, running into the tent.

"Hey little man," Jejune smiles, crouching down for a hug. She holds him for a long time. "Why didn't you wait for me?"

"It wasn't far," he says, releasing from their embrace.

"You were alright walking by yourself," she asks, stroking his hair.

"Yup," he beams. "I'm independent!"

"Oh, new word you learned?"

"Indeed, I.N.D.E.E.D." he spells. Stevey turns to me as Jejune continues to caress his hair. "Hi Rose, how –" he stops, his smile disappearing as his green eyes scan my spheres. Stevey approaches me, my numb eyes following his path as he reaches my side. He grips his skinny arms around my waist, squeezing his small face into me. "It's okay."

Although simple, those two words send a tsunami of sadness throughout my body. I look to Jejune, adjusting her hat as she shields her face. Cast in a shadow, her eyes faintly glisten with water. I look down as Stevey continues to hug me. This journey has been hard on all of us, not just me. Clenching my eyes shut, I strain to keep my emotions under control. Stevey will never know it, but this hug and those two words were all I needed to hear. Stevey is right, it's okay. At this exact moment, I may not feel okay, but I will be. I will be okay.

I am bored. I should be thankful for the relaxation after the craziness of our journey to arrive here, I just need something to do. As promised, Jejune took Stevey further up the mountains yesterday. Not wanting to tarnish Stevey's experience with Jejune and I's unresolved conversation, I did not join. I did however meet up after for communal dinner.

Although we have been here a few days, I am still adjusting to the change. As for Jejune and Stevey, they have a routine. With the river, Jejune wakes up before the sun rises and goes to work like she did in Amella. With the kids, Stevey goes to school and learns just like he did in Amella. As for me, I do not know what to do.

With Jejune and Stevey gone, I decided to attend communal breakfast; I cannot be alone all day. Unfortunately, Wila arrived at the same time and I could not say no when she invited me to sit with her. It is not that I do not like her, but after our last breakfast together, I keep my answers short and avoid asking any questions.

"Do you have any plans for today?" Wila asks as we finish our last bites. Chewing on my food, I shake my head. "Do you want to help me clean?"

"Sure," I say, rising from my seat.

"Meet me by the buffet." She clutches her sky blue floral necklace. "I'll get the carts." Grabbing my plate, I head towards the buffet. Waiting for Wila to return, I realize how small Cali is; I am able to see everything within it. It is drastically different than the North. The only similarity is there are no public clocks. In Cali however, the sun and moon are your timekeepers. "Apologies," Wila exhales, struggling to roll two wooden carts our way. "I'm sure you aren't used to this heat."

"Not yet," I say, taking a cart from her.

"Thank you so much for the help Rose." Wila carefully places the trays of leftover food in her cart. "I really appreciate it."

"Of course," I smile, doing the same.

"Forest usually helps but he's working in the gardens early today." Weaving in and out like lab rats in a maze, Wila and I clear off each table, slowly making our way to the work station tents. "You wouldn't mind helping with the dishes either would you?" Small drops of sweat outline her gray hair.

"Not at all." Continuing on, I glance at each station we pass. Sewing, woodworking, gardens. Wila stops at the greenhouse, peeking inside, squinting to get a better view. She turns with a small grin on her face.

"Just wanted to check on Forest," she whispers. I follow, also peering into the greenhouse. Forest is working over fresh wet soil, his fingers massaging the charcoal dirt. "Forest has been spending a lot of time in there," Wila continues, pushing her cart through a tent in front of us. "Must be working on something new. He loves his role. Have you found your role?"

"No," I shout, catching up to Wila. This is a tent we did not see on our tour. It resembles a kitchen with two large sinks, a wooden island in the middle, and a wall of shelves. One shelf is empty, while the others are stacked with an abundance of lopsided dishes, bowls, utensils, and pots and pans.

"What did you do before coming to Cali?" Following Wila's lead, I watch as she takes the plates we have gathered off her cart and into the sink.

"Film Industry," I answer. I turn on my faucet, the running of both our sinks filling the silence.

"Was that… rewarding?" Wila asks, continuing to clean her dishes.

"It was a job," I shrug, placing my first washed dish on the counter.

"Good." Wila states, a small smile on her aged face. "Hopefully you can find a rewarding role here." We both face our heads down to clean.

"What is your role?" I ask.

"Why this is my role," she smiles. "I used to be a doctor, but my memory is not so great anymore." Nodding, I think of what to ask next.

"What is Cali's role? The leader or something?"

"No," Wila scoffs, placing a couple washed utensils on the island, her glacier blue and cream shawl swaying. "We're a community, no hierarchy."

"What is her role then?" Wila remains quiet, scraping food into a barrel next to her before responding.

"She keeps Cali alive." Wila looks to me, her cloudy cobalt eyes locking with mine. "She's wonderful." Our conversation goes quiet as we continue to wash dishes. With our carts empty, we turn off the faucets. "We'll dry these and put them on the shelves." Wila hands me a towel. I stare at the fabric detailed with rich red and gold trim accents.

"This is the prettiest dish towel I have ever seen," I state, examining the soft material.

"The sewers here do a beautiful job," she comments, delicately drying the plates in front of her. "But this one is my favorite." She stops drying her dish and hands me her towel. My eyes focus on a large W embroidered over marble blue fabric. "My favorite color," she admits, gesturing to her blue necklace and clothing. "My granddaughter Ivy made it for me."

"She made this?" I question, handing back the towel.

"Yes," she remarks, staring at the W on the towel. "A very talented young

41

girl. She's joined the sewers since she could walk."

"So Ivy grew up here?" I inquire.

"Yes, we all did."

"All?"

"Yes, three generations," Wila joyfully states. "Myself, my son Forest, and now my granddaughter Ivy."

"How long have you been here?"

"Oh my," she laughs, placing her plate and towel on the table, searching for an answer. "At least thirty years." I halt wiping the dish in front of me.

"Thirty years?" I ask puzzled. Cali has been here for that long? How has no one in Amella heard of this place before?

"This was sand when we got here, nothing but desert. Cali has done so much to build our community." Tearing up, her boney hands reach out. A chill scurries up my arms as her cold palms press against mine. "I'm beyond grateful for what she's provided." She blinks as a single tear slides down her face, rolling over her dark makeup without smudging it. "Especially given what she's been through." Wila delicately dabs her fingers under her eyelids, sniffles, then goes back to drying. Feeling confident on how much Wila has already opened up to me, I investigate more.

"Been through?" I ask. Wila's hand slowly spins to a stop, like a record when it reaches the end of a track.

"Just an awful time," Wila whispers. "When we were in Amella, we all, well Cali, had a falling –"

"Granny!" I whip my head around to see a young girl run into the tent.

"Ivy, honey," Wila smiles. "Why aren't you in school?"

"I am!" she sings. "I made you this in class today!" Ivy shoots forward her arms, presenting a floral crown.

"It's wonderful," Wila cheers, bowing her head. Ivy wiggles on her tippy toes, placing the crown on top of her silver hair.

"I used Wila flowers for your name and Mayflowers because daddy said those flowers are from where you used to live." Wila stares intensely at Ivy. Matching the flowers surrounding her head, Wila's face becomes white.

"Forest told you this?" I watch as Wila mirrors Ivy's movement, both their heads nodding as their darkened eyes stare at one another. "Well, it's lovely." Ivy gives her grandmother a hug before she runs back out of the tent.

"She is very talented," I remark, scanning over her floral crown.

"Yes very," Wila forcibly smiles. "Will you excuse me for a moment." Wila clutches onto her necklace, quietly making her exit. Confused, I watch her leave as she continues to fidget with her necklace.

Alone, I dry the remaining utensils. My eyes wander to Wila's towel, the bold W grabbing my attention. I sneak one last glance at Wila before she leaves the tent, eyeing her new floral crown. Mayflowers. I have never heard of a Mayflower in the North. Could they grow in a different State? Wila did say she was in Amella. Did she used to live in Amella with Cali? And what was Wila about to say. An awful time, something happened to Cali. What could have happened to make her leave Amella? My mind stops, coming to another alarming conclusion. Maybe it was not voluntary. Maybe Cali did not choose to leave. Maybe Cali was forced to leave.

***

The next three days were once again underwhelming. Of course, I am happy Jejune and Stevey are finding their way in this new place, but with no Film Industry, I have nothing to do. Although the original plan was to discover this mysterious piece of land then head back to Amella, I guess in some respect we are safer here. It seems Cali knows of Amella but Amella does not know of Cali. For now, this works in our favor after fleeing Counting Day. Crew members cannot capture us if they do not know our hiding place even exists.

Yesterday I did explore more of the mountain trail and got to see my first real sunset. The scarlet sun, bronze mountain tops, blue solar panels, mixed with the plum and indigo sky. You would think the clash of colors would form a disconnect, but they all worked to create a short time of beauty. Planning to see the sunset again today, Wila reminded me at breakfast that the ceremony is tonight. I did not believe her at first, but then I realized it has been a week. I feel like we just crash landed in Cali. I am actually looking forward to attending tonight to spend time with Jejune and Stevey. I may not be a fan of the ceremony, but I miss spending time with the both of them. Even if we do not participate, it will be nice to not go alone, or be stuck another minute with Wila.

I waited a good while for Jejune to return from work. Once the moon re-placed the sun in the sky, I realized she may have gone straight to the ceremony. As predicted, I arrive to see Jejune sharing a bench with a few other fishermen. Before I can get Jejune's attention, Wila waves, gesturing for me to join her and Forest. Finally, I look back to Jejune, patting the open spot next to her. Avoiding Wila's attempt, I walk by the hot fire to meet Jejune.

"Thanks for saving me a seat," I smile. Tilting my head, I point to Jejune's head as I sit on the warm bench.

"Oh yeah," she laughs, feeling for the floral crown placed over her JJ hat. "Stevey made it in school the other day. Begged me to show it off tonight."

"I can see," my eyes scanning the crowd all with floral crowns. "Guess I did not get the memo."

"Oh shit," Jejune says, taking notice of everyone else's head. "I'll have Ste-vey make one for you to wear next ceremony." She snaps her fingers, a smirk across her face. "He can make one with roses for your name."

"Or sunflowers to match your hair," the guy next to her adds. Jejune and the others nod in agreement. I faintly smile, forgetting that my hair is no longer brown.

"Speaking of," I lean forward looking behind her. "Where is Stevey?"

"With the other kids," Jejune nudges her head. I turn to see an open tent full of kids. "Cali said tonight's challenge might bring up dark memories for people."

"You guys got dark secrets?" the guy next to her snickers, his face barely shown in the light of the fire. "Maybe you'll get your marks tonight."

"Sure Oliver," Jejune scoffs, rolling her eyes. Before I can ask Jejune how her day was, the circle grows quiet. Similar to last week's ceremony, Cali emerges, her orange hair matching the movements of the flames. Fumbling, Jejune and I join in standing with the rest of the circle. On Cali's command, we all sit as she begins.

"Welcome to our ceremony. The circle of crying ceremony." As if reading from a script, Cali recites the same speech. "This is a safe space. Share your grief, your sadness, your pain. We're here to listen and cry together. Tonight, our challenge is hurt." Unlike last week, no one comments. Utter silence. "A time you were hurt. A time you felt the most hurt. A time you were at your lowest." Cali's crunching of pebbles stops as she stands a few feet from our bench. Twinkling from the fire, her eyes stay glued to Jejune. "Last ceremony I felt pain from you Jejune," she proclaims over the open air. "Do you want to share that pain?"

"No thanks," Jejune exhales.

"Generally, people who attend the ceremony participate in the ceremony." Assisting in Cali's argument, others nod as Oliver shoves Jejune.

"Alright," Jejune states, throwing her hands up in surrender. "I was hurt when," she closes her eyes. Nervous, I study Jejune's face, wondering what she will share. "When I fell down the hill to get here." The tension in my shoulders loosens as I hold in a laugh. Classic Jejune. "I mean it really hurt when I landed." A smile creeps on her face. Not able to hold it, I cover my mouth as Jejune laughs loudly, echoing with the crackling fire.

"Hilarious," Cali states. "Using humor to cope."

"I'm not coping, it really hurt!" She looks to me. Ceasing my laughter, I raise my eyebrows. It is obvious Cali, along with the rest of the circle, do not find Jejune's sarcasm laughable. "These people don't find anything funny," she mumbles towards me.

"The ceremony isn't meant for senseless foolishness," Cali scorns. Clearing her throat, Jejune turns back to face everyone. "If you can't respect that, then you can leave."

"No, I respect it," Jejune reassures.

"Then share your real pain," Cali rebuttals. A seriousness washes over the circle as the wind picks up. The flame from the fire flaps as Cali remains still, waiting for Jejune. Shoving her again, Oliver pushes Jejune's arm.

"Okay fine," Jejune slaps her hands loudly on her thighs. Jejune swallows, shifting her body weight slightly. She looks to me, a sense of vulnerability in her eyes. I nod to Jejune, as if I am giving her approval to share. Jejune is usually the strong one, so why am I the one telling her to have courage. "It isn't a long tale. Dad died, I got upset, tried to cut it out," pointing to her scar. "Couldn't cut it out, now I got a scar for life. That's it."

"That's it," Cali states.

"That's it," Jejune sternly says. Eyes flicking down, Jejune avoids everyone's focus on her. I stare at Jejune. Why did she not tell me that story before?

"How did your dad die?" Cali asks.

"A fishing accident coming from the other side of town." Jejune sneaks a glance towards me.

"It was an accident?"

"Yup."

"So why did you inflict pain on yourself," a woman blurts out across the fire. "It wasn't your fault." Others look towards Jejune, mirroring the pain in her eyes. Jejune frowns, the somberness erasing from her face.

"Young and dumb," she laughs. "Feeling rebellious."

47

"Is that how you came here," Oliver questions. "Feeling rebellious?"

"I guess you could say so," she nods towards him.

"So coming here wasn't by accident," Cali chimes in.

"Nope, no such thing as accidents."

"But your dad died –"

"I thought the topic was on hurt?" Jejune asks, cutting Cali off.

"Apologies," Cali confesses. "I'm nearly trying to make the connection between losing someone dear to you and running away." Jejune leans back, her eyebrows furrowing with confusion.

"Running away?" she repeats.

"Yes, running away from the environment where your dad had his accident. Right?" Cali begins circling the fire, looking for agreement from others. "Or was it not an accident and there's another reason why you're running." Cali stops walking, standing frozen, staring at Jejune. As her red scar shines off the fire, Jejune waves her finger at Cali, a grin forming on her face.

"I can see," she laughs. "I can see why you run this whole thing. You're good with your words." Like watching a tennis match, my eyes shift back and forth between Cali and Jejune.

"Was your dad's death an accident?" Cali softly asks. The silence is long as Jejune hesitates to respond, the wind howling around us.

"No." Shocked, my eyes stay locked on Jejune. "He was killed."

What is she doing?

"Killed by –"

"By Amella," she spits. Light gasps emit from people around the circle. My bones fill with panic. Why would she admit the truth? Jejune stares blankly into the fire as Oliver rests his hand on her shoulder, providing her comfort. Jejune blinks and as her eyelids meet, a drop of water sneaks out of her eye, splashing against her leg. I have never seen Jejune cry.

"Amella doesn't have to control you anymore," Cali says, approaching Jejune. She stands above her, hand already caked in dark makeup. "You can stop running. It is time." Jejune tilts her head up, her face looking to Cali.

"Do it," Jejune states. Cali's hand connects under Jejune's eye, smearing the dark makeup Jejune swore to never wear. All clap and chant the vanishing spheres phrase as Cali dips her thumb in the bowl again, doing the same for her other eye. Numb, I come back to reality when I hear my name. Slowly, I look up to Cali.

"Would you like to share?" she asks. Still in shock, my eyes look to Jejune. With her white spheres and crimson scar shielded by the dark makeup, the emerald tint in her eyes vividly shines. I remain entranced with her.

"Um," I clear my throat. "The first time I felt hurt was recently." Heart pounding, my eyes lock on Jejune. Of course, my story is nowhere near as profound as Jejune's, no one could top that. But if Jejune, the most reserved person I know can share and accept a stranger erasing her spheres, I guess I can too. "I was a six. Never cried before. I had many things bottling up inside me but," I pause, my face hot as I stare at Jejune. "Someone close to me broke my heart, and that was what made me let it all out." My story sits in the air as I stare at Jejune, continuing to perceive her new face.

"Incredible," Cali says. "Years of not crying. A true six." Cali dips her finger in the bowl, her dark thumb hovering in front of my face. I look up at her, accepting my fate. "It is time," she announces. Unblinking, we continue to stare at one another as her thumb drags across my skin. I watch Cali's lips separate as she speaks, but hear nothing. I feel Jejune and others clap near me, but still hear nothing. My ears ring the same as when the guns went off on the dock. Cali moves onto my next eye, forcefully and urgently smearing the makeup. As Cali lifts her finger off my face, my hearing comes back, like someone unmuting a television. My senses swell with pressure as a crowd swarms around us.

Blinking to regain my bearings, members of Cali bombard Jejune and I. Hugging us. Holding us. Thanking us. The backlight of the fire creates a haunting image of hazy shadows and silhouettes towering over us. Like a wave receding, people move away from me and surround Jejune.

I watch people flaunt over Jejune. Their eyes filling with tears. Their hands shaking with compassion. Their faces melting with immense empathy. Jejune is met with celebration, triumph, encouragement. Whereas I, it was almost an obligation, as if people felt they had to address me before moving on to the person they truly want to recognize. I feel like an outcast as more people connect with Jejune, ignoring my presence right beside her. Embarrassed, my mind replays the story I told. How miniscule the hurt in my tale was versus Jejune's. Life is a competition, and it always will be. As of now, Jejune is winning. I used to be a six, the greatest honor in Amella, but here, everything is different. Here in Cali, there is no scoring system. My points do not matter. My spheres do not matter. Most of all, in Cali, I do not matter.

Sleep did not greet me after the ceremony. My mind was acutely alert making my eyes unable to shut. Worst of all, I did not get to talk to Jejune. With Stevey around, Jejune maximized her time with him, making it clear to not approach her regarding the ceremony. I understood and respected her wishes, but my brain would not relax, craving for an explanation from Jejune to help ease my mind. I did not care about Jejune's story. All I cared about was why. Why did she not feel comfortable telling me about her scar? Why did I not earn her trust? As the morning sun seeps through our tent, I am now left wondering why Jejune is avoiding me.

Jejune has the same routine. Quick shower. Help Stevey get ready. Eat breakfast. Head out. This morning, it is a totally different procedure. All Jejune did was help Stevey get ready. No shower. No food. Just wake up and go. I cannot help but feel this change is directed towards me. Attempting to get an ounce of rest, I close my eyes, focusing on steadying my breathing. With no luck, I drag my exhausted body into the shower.

My eyes remain closed as the warm water kisses my skin, relaxing my tense muscles. Groggily I rub my eye but immediately yank my hand away, springing my eyes open to see the damage. Puzzled, I wipe under my eye again and look to my hand. All I see is the crinkling of my pruney fingertips. Using both hands, I furiously scrub under both eyes, tugging at my skin rapidly. I look to my hands again as water leaks off my face, my curiosity instantly becoming concern.

Hurling the curtain open, I turn off the shower and rush out, my naked body stinging with coolness. My hand swipes across the mirror, erasing the fogginess to show my damp face still with the dark makeup. Not smudged. Not running. Leaning over the sink, the cold porcelain pinches my bare hipbones. My fingers slap under my eyes, pulling down the skin with each finger, like a guitarist strumming their instrument. Breathing deeply, my nervous exhales fog the mirror as I stand still. The dark makeup does... nothing. It is sticking to my skin, refusing to leave. My palms rest on my cheeks as I remain fixated on my reflection.

Heart pounding, my eyes widen as I rise on my toes, getting as close as I can to the mirror. Carefully, I use both my pointer fingers, spreading the tender skin attached to my spheres. I stretch my skin until it stings, watching as my hidden spheres bulge under the makeup, trying to break free. I fall back on my heels, dropping my hands to give the skin under my eyes relief.

Is this makeup permanent?

I stare at my face, the dark makeup making my brown eyes as jet black as my pupils. Just when I thought this week could not get any more bizarre. A shiver sprints up my spine as I reach for my towel. I dry off and take one last glance at the person in my reflection. Blonde hair. Dark eyes. No spheres.

Blinking hard, I turn away from the mirror and move on with my day. Hastily, I throw on a shirt and shorts. I need to get to breakfast. I have been going every morning. If I do not go, it will not only look suspicious, but Wila will probably come looking for me. She means well, but the last thing I need is her snooping around our tent. Hopping into my shoes, I move the tent entrance open and bump into Cali.

"Good morning Rose," she sings. "How did you sleep?"

"Morning," I say, forcing a smile. "Fine."

"Do you have anything scheduled for today?" I stare into her round doe eyes, knowing that she is fully aware I have nothing to do here.

"Just breakfast."

"Wonderful," she smiles, scrunching her aged cheeks. "Before that, would you join me for a stroll. I would love to talk." Despite exhaustion screaming throughout my body, I agree. Following the path out of the living quarters, Cali nods and smiles to people milling about.

"Are you a natural blonde?" Cali asks suddenly. She keeps her head down, her eyes glancing in my direction. Examining her makeup, I try to see any creases or smudges, but just like mine, I find no faults.

"No," I confess. "Brunette. You?"

"Oh dear," she giggles, twisting her fingers in her long hair. "All natural here. The sun has lightened it over the years though." My eyes follow her wavy hair from the top of her floral crown to the fine strands tapping her hips. I have never even grown my hair past my shoulders.

Our conversation goes quiet as we head to the base of the mountain, Cali's musical beads mingling with the sawing of the tree workers. Cali stops, gesturing to a bench just before the mountain trail. She brushes her long shawl underneath her as we sit. Still wondering why she dragged me all the way out here to talk, I watch as Cali joyfully overlooks Cali.

"Breathtaking isn't it," she exhales. "It truly is a wild yet wonderful world we live in. It's magical." Coming out of her trance, she faces me, slowly reaching above her. "Nature is a gift." She massages the leaves on the trees arching over us. "We don't want to disturb nature."

"Aren't you disturbing it by being here," I hear my own voice say.

Crap, I thought I said that just in my head.

Swallowing, I watch Cali, her fingers tensing around the leaves, pinching them harshly. She breathes in deeply, looking to me with a smile.

"I do apologize we don't have a Film Industry in Cali," she states, ignoring my nature comment. "We don't have a need for propaganda." Speaking of, I need to ask how she knows my occupation. "However," she continues, stopping my train of thought. "I'd like you to work on a special project with me, would you be open to that?" A special project? I contemplate my answer as the tree workers continue to loudly chop in the distance.

"What is the project." Turning forward to face all of Cali, she places her hands on her thighs, spine straight as a flag pole.

"I feel as though you don't trust me, and I want to build our trust."

"Just getting used to a new environment," I frown.

"Understandable," Cali nods in recognition. "You're not home, but hopefully, this can be your home." She turns, a smile on her face.

"Home is with my mom and dad." Our darkened eyes stare at one another. Not responding, she stands, gliding past my body on the bench.

"Come," she orders. Weaving through vibrant plants complimenting the ombre mountains surrounding us, the sound of the workers fades away as we immerse ourselves deeper with nature. "I couldn't sense your energy," Cali admits. "Now Jejune, she's been through pain, but you haven't. Your story was not pain, that was pity. You felt bad for yourself." I stare at Cali, taking in her judgment. "That isn't pain, but maybe one day, you'll feel true pain." Before I can respond, Cali spins around, tilting her head extremely far back, hair stretching past her butt.

"Look at the sky," she instructs. Confused, I follow Cali's head, squinting slightly. "So beautiful, yet no one appreciates it. We take it for granted, except when it's not there. Clouds or the darkness of night. Then we appreciate it, then we want it. Then when it returns, we act like we did before, ignore it." I bring my neck to its natural position, impressed Cali is able to arch her back for this long at her age. "But one day it may always be cloudy, always be darkness. Look in front of you and realize what you have Rose, because one day, it might not be there." Cali breaks her trance from the sky and looks towards me. "So appreciate it."

I nod, acknowledging her odd monologue. I am getting the sense Cali is a fan of speeches. As I remain consumed by greenery, Cali starts towards the flat, sandy ground.

"What about you," I shout, stopping Cali in her tracks. "When did you first feel true pain?" Cali turns around, gently clasping her hands in front of her.

"Another ceremony." She forces a smile, resuming her walk.

"And this special project," I say, raising my eyebrows. Stopping again, Cali waits a beat. After what feels like a lifetime, she swivels her head, her boney cheeks and large eyes scanning me.

"Tomorrow." She faces her head straight, leaving me to look at her ginger, honey hair. "Let's start fresh tomorrow."

Special project? What project is so special Cali needs just me? Tired of the blazing sun, I march back to our tent; no point in getting breakfast now. I slip my shoes off, my sweaty toes squishing over the thick carpet. Cooling my core temperature, I grab a cup, filling it with cold water. Slumping on the couch, I gulp down my drink, the icy liquid infusing my warm gums. Just as relaxation is kicking in, my eyes see the tent curtain open.

"Morning," Jejune states, taken aback. "I thought you'd be at breakfast." She continues to the kitchen, tossing her bag on the counter. Opening the fridge, her dark makeup glows from the light, the flowers around her hat shifting with the air.

"Not today," I answer as she closes the fridge. Why was she shocked to see me? Did she plan to come back when I was not around? Rising from the comfy cushions, I walk towards the kitchen. Sitting on the stool across from her, I place my empty cup on the counter. "Are we good?"

"Yeah, why wouldn't we be," she says, continuing to pack her bag. Before I can respond, she turns around, riffling through the cabinets.

"I feel like you are avoiding me." Nervous, I sit, waiting for Jejune's response. I know we are best friends, but right now, I feel like the title of 'friends' is a stretch; we are merely passing roommates.

"How so?" she questions, closing the cabinets. She stuffs her bag some more then glances in my direction. Disappearing under her hat, she raises her eyebrows waiting for my answer.

"You left in such a hurry this morning."

"Yeah, to get Stevey's glasses fixed before school." Makes sense, I guess she was not trying to steer clear of me after all.

"Why didn't you tell me?" I ask, changing the subject.

"Tell you…" she frowns, keeping eye contact with me. A sadness consumes me. She does not even know what I am talking about.

"About your scar. After all these years I thought you would have opened up to me instead of them," I state, gesturing out towards where the ceremony was held.

"Never came up," she shrugs. Hurt, my eyes sink down. "Damn," she laughs, jolting my eyes back up. "Who would have thought in one week you and I would have a complete makeover." I look her up and down. Floral crown. Dark eyes. Sage overalls. Why is she joking? How is she finding anything about our conversation funny. Fed up, I raise my voice.

"Jejune what is going on with you."

"I'm happy," she smiles. "For the first time in a long time I'm happy."

"Happy?" I ask, my face twisting with confusion.

"This place is pretty sweet."

"I think you're getting a little too comfortable."

"I think you're just mad you don't fit in," she mumbles.

"Fit in? You said you wanted to find a better place than Amella –"

"And this is better," she says. "No curfew, no points, and Stevey has friends. *Friends*, Rose." Finished in the kitchen, Jejune drags her bag off the counter and into the hallway. I keep my mouth shut. At the end of the day, it is never about what Jejune wants, it is always what Stevey wants. If Stevey is happy, Jejune is happy.

"Cali thinks that I don't trust her," I confess.

"Well, do you?" she asks, rummaging through her clothes.

"I don't know. She's having me do a special task to gain her trust."

"That's great," Jejune smiles, coming back into the main room.

"No Jejune I —"

"I gotta go, the boat's leaving in ten." Zipping her bag, she slides it on her shoulder. "We'll talk later." Adjusting the floral crown on her hat, she heads outside.

"Jejune," I spit. She stops, leaning her head forward, waiting for me to continue. My numb body stares at her as my mind rages. I want to scream at her. I want to fight like we usually do when we disagree. Yell back and forth. Shout out opinions. Get on each other's nerves. At least then I would know Jejune cares enough to have a real conversation with me. Now there is only silence as Jejune's dark eyes look to me, her radiant scar no longer able to pierce through me. "Be safe."

"Will do," she winks, officially leaving me to my new normal. Alone.

***

Jejune, Oliver, and the other fishers came back just in time for communal dinner. Guess there were not too many fish to catch today. Although I get to spend a meal with Jejune and Stevey, I neglect adding to the conversation with the other fishers around. It is nice to be included, but I still feel like an outsider. Especially with Jejune's comment of how I do not fit in. Maybe she is right. I nibble on my food as I watch Jejune and Stevey laugh together. Jejune does look happy. Happier than she ever did in Amella, and she is still working in a role she loves. I may not want the role of this special project, but it might be my only option. I cannot possibly continue to do nothing each day. I need to find out more about Cali. Cali the place and more specifically Cali the person. If agreeing to this special project is it, then so be it. Smiling, I raise my cup slightly to myself. Wila said we have to do our part here in Cali, and I guess I found it. Cheers to me and my future role: Cali's secret special project.

V. ANGELO

Confident. This morning I am waking up confident. Tired of feeling sorry for myself, I am looking at today with a new mindset. A mindset of optimism. Flinging our tent open, I inhale deeply, taking in the start of a fresh, new day. With a skip in my step, I follow the sandy path to the buffet area. After stacking my plate high with protein, I find the familiar faces of Wila and Forest. Today, I gladly join them for breakfast.

"Rose, could you help me with the dishes today?" Wila kindly asks.

"Actually," I smile. "I can't. I have a role." Wila's eyes widen, her face overcome with joy. She taps Forest gently on the shoulder. "Did you hear that Forest, Rose has a role." Chewing his food, Forest keeps his head down, silently nodding. "Congratulations," she sings. "What's your role?"

"I am not sure what the official title is, but I will be working on a special project." Forest snaps his head up, our eyes meeting for the first time.

"Special project," he repeats, maintaining eye contact with me. Never hearing Forest speak before, his voice is much deeper than I imagined. As our eyes meet for the first time, I nod, continuing to study his face.

"Yes," Wila whispers, leaning her head in towards Forest. "A special project." Forest's dark eyes continue to stare through me, processing Wila's words.

Abruptly he stands, searching the breakfast area. Following his movements, my brows furrow with confusion as I watch him trudge towards Cali. Forest stops, his strongly built body blocking my view of Cali.

"It is a great fit," Wila states behind me, my focus still on Forest. Wila's clammy hands connect with mine, reverting my attention back to her. "It is a great fit. Your new role. You'll be perfect."

"Thanks," I reply, forcing a smile. Sliding my hands out of her reach, I lean back and turn around. Perplexed, my eyes see Forest and Cali gone.

"So," Cali states, now inches away from our table. My heart skips a beat as I nervously exhale. "Guess you heard the good news."

"We did," Wila says. "Perfect choice Cali." As my heart steadies to a normal beat, I tune Wila and Cali out, twisting my neck. My eyes rapidly scour the area for any sign of Forest. I face the table when I hear my name.

"Right Rose," Cali questions. Clearing my throat, I grab my drink.

"Right," I agree, taking a long sip.

"Well, I don't want to rush you but we do have to get started," Cali states, clasping her hands in front of her garments.

"I'll clean your plate," Wila smiles, her aged skin crinkling.

"Thanks," I reply. Leaving the breakfast area, Cali and I walk side by side towards the work stations. Her thin layered clothes blow in my direction, the soft fabric petting my legs. Ceasing our silence, I speak. "Wila said I am the perfect fit."

"Indeed you are," Cali smiles.

"What would that fit be exactly?"

"You'll be assisting in Cali's product supplies."

"So not self sustaining in every aspect," I state, gesturing to the work stations in front of us.

"Self sustaining to a point. You couldn't possibly think we have everything we need here. You'll be helping with the trade run." Cali steps in front of me, a smile growing on her face. "Kind of like film. Organization, scheduling, gathering equipment, before the lights, camera, action!"

"Sure," I say. "About that," I add. "How did you know I worked in the Film Industry?"

"Why you told me," Cali quickly replies, continuing on.

"I didn't," I correct, catching up to her. "Only Jejune told you her occupation when we arrived." My curious eyes focus on Cali as she keeps her head down, her thin hair blocking her face. Waiting for a response, my body tenses with anticipation.

"Your makeup," she turns her head, finally making eye contact with me. "I assumed with your makeup. Only actresses in the Film Industry wear makeup." Cali looks back forward. "The trade run is next week," she says, changing the subject. "Today our product focus will be bamboo."

"Um," I reply, trying to focus on the current conversation topic. "Are we making the products?"

"No, just rounding up what we already have," she states, her voice drowned out as we pass the sewing machines. I follow Cali, her shawl acting as an ombre trail pulling me along. As my ears fill with a symphony of sounds from the work stations, my eyes stop my movement when we walk by the greenhouse. To my surprise the greenhouse is empty. No Forest?

"Is Forest okay?" I shout towards Cali, jogging to reach her side.

"Who?" Cali questions, tilting her head. "Oh Forest, he's fine," she scoffs, entering the tent Wila and I cleaned dishes in the other day. Cali exhales, a stillness washing over her face. "Forest worked on the special project with me but it wasn't a good fit. I think he's jealous you took his role." Took it? I was given the role. "If he gives you any trouble," she says, gently tapping my arm. "Please don't hesitate to let me know." I swallow as Cali's delicate fingers stay connected to my bare arm.

"You mentioned the trade run is next week?" I ask.

"Yes!" Cali beams, drifting away and heading towards the shelves jam packed with bamboo items. "We're on a time crunch but," her thin lips spreading widely into a grin. "With your help we can get it done."

"Okay," I nod, joining Cali at the shelves. "Just tell me what to do."

"Splendid." Nudging her head, she moves to the other side of the tent. "We need to take these," she opens the curtain to reveal crates stacked in an orderly fashion, "out of here so we can fill them with those," she states, pointing to the shelves.

"That is it?" I question.

"That's it," she smiles. "For now, at least." Following Cali's lead, I join her in grabbing one wooden crate at a time, walking each back into the center of the tent.

Within no time, Cali and I have a solid routine. After bringing the crates in the tent, we supply each one with various items. Utensils, plates, bowls, cutting boards, a carnival of bamboo. The task is tedious, yet enjoyable. Still skeptical why I was the 'perfect fit' for organizing supplies into shipment crates, I guess I should not complain. I am not in the blaring sun. I am not surrounded by constant noises on a film set. I am content as I work. More importantly, Cali is not judging or staring me down. For the first time since arriving here, I feel busy. Useful even, like I am finally accepted and wanted. I understand now what Wila meant when she said we are a part of Cali and have to do our part. I do feel like I am a part of Cali, and surprisingly, I do not feel like I have to do my part, but I want to do my part.

"Do you have a hat?"

"No," I respond.

"Oh dear," Cali sighs, standing at the front of our tent. "We'll see if the sewers have any on hand." Closing the opening to the tent, I follow her down the path out of the living quarters. Thank goodness Cali is a slow walker, my thighs and back are aching from bending and lifting supplies yesterday. My body has not been in this much pain since Jejune, Stevey, and I's travels through the woods.

As we pass the ceremony area, Stevey's class is scattered about for an out-door lesson. His tiny fingers wave at me and I wave back, my cheeks lifting with a smile. Not knowing when our special project work was going to start this morning, I woke up earlier than usual. In doing so, I was able to have breakfast with Jejune and Stevey. Eating in the kitchen, it was enjoyable to share a meal just the three of us, like old times. Stevey brought us up to speed on everything he is learning in school, but most of all, how excited he is to be making friends. I wave at Stevey until he turns away, joining his classmates in their lesson again.

"Good morning Lily," Cali says to a teenage girl at a sewing machine.

"Good morning!" Her delicate hands pause feeding fabric further through the machine. "Looking for new garments," she asks, directing her attention to me.

"Not quite. Do you have any hats we can borrow?"

"Of course," she pushes her chair back, leading us into the tent. "We're re-stocked. Pick your favorite," she instructs, pointing to a wall of hung up hats.

"Wow," I state, observing the mass selection. By default, I go with the hat closest to me, reaching out towards the brown cap.

"Come on now!" Cali grabs the hat from my hands, placing it back on the hanger. "You can pick a better one than that."

Trying again, my eyes rescan each hat. Blue, red, purple, camouflage, tie dye; my sight is overwhelmed with the rainbow before me. Not wanting to drag it out, I select a green safari hat.

"Good choice," Lily says. "Keep your neck covered as well."

"Indeed," Cali agrees, selecting a floral patterned safari hat. "Now pick five more." Confused, I quickly do as I am told. "Thank you Lily." Cali grabs a handful herself as I secure my hat on and follow her out the tent.

"Seems like the sewers had plenty of hats on hand," I state.

"Yes," Cali replies, shimmying her floral crown over her floral hat creating a kaleidoscope of petals. "Smart thinking on the safari hat style."

"So why are hats needed for today?" I question, flipping through the pile in my hands. Making our way to the ceremony area, we approach an empty bench opposite of the school children.

"Today our focus is syrup. We'll be helping the tree workers collect as much as we can." I turn around to see the tree workers sawing away, the faint voices of Stevey's class echoing behind me. So much for avoiding the blaring sun. "This is all in prep for the trade run," she continues, drawing my attention back to her. "We gather supplies that we have in Cali in exchange for supplies that we don't have."

"A bartering system."

"Precisely," Cali smiles, the shade from our hats making her dark eyes even darker. "This run we'll trade three items. Bamboo, syrup, and honey."

"And what does Cali get in return?"

"Let's let that be a surprise," Cali grins. Unclear why she cannot just tell me, I smile back confused. "But now, syrup!" She stands, clapping her hands loudly. "Are they ready?" Cali shouts across the ceremony area.

"They sure are!" Stevey's teacher sings. I snap my head to Stevey's class as they bombard Cali and I.

"Now children," Cali proclaims. "We get what we get and we don't get upset, right?" The students nod their heads quickly. Stunned, I fumble with the hats in my hands as Stevey and four other classmates approach me.

"Can I *please* have the green one?" Stevey loudly whispers. Winking, I hand Stevey the green hat. Like a pogo stick, his body bounces with excitement as he shimmies the oversized hat on his tiny head. Grinning, I hand out the rest to the other classmates, each thanking me with their dark eyes.

"Children this is Rose." Cali gestures to me. "She's going to join us for your lesson today. Who can tell us what that would be?" The class shoots their arms up, many wiggling on their tippy toes. Cali looks to me to choose a student to share.

"Oh," I say, caught off guard. "Stevey?" I pick.

"Our lesson was on syrup. S.Y.R.U.P." he quickly spells, a giggle escaping his huge smile. "We learned it comes from trees and you do something called tapping to get syrup out."

"Excellent!" Cali cheers. "Great work Miss Meadow." Stevey's teacher smiles, her short curls framing her face. "Let's get started!" Not able to contain their excitement, Stevey and his classmates run to the tree workers. "Miss Meadow's class will be assisting us with the syrup gathering today," Cali informs me. "Thankfully, spring is ending so we only have one tree to tap for this trade run. You and I will have less work to do but the children still get to learn." Miss Meadow attempts to calm down the class as Cali leads the way to a tree where a worker is already waiting.

"Here come my helpers!" the man hollers. The stampede of students comes to a halt, the majority of them resembling a pack of racoons with their undereye dark makeup. "We ready to tap a tree for syrup?"

"Yes!" Stevey's class cheers.

"Let's first see if this tree is big enough to tap from. Two at a time come and hug the tree." Taking turns, the students wrap their small arms around the tree, laughing nonstop. "Who knows what we have to do next?"

"Drill!" a student shouts.

"Correct, but I'll be doing that one, don't want you kids getting hurt." Reaching down, he grabs a drill, angling the tool up as he slowly punctures the tree. In unison, the class covers their ears, continuing to watch the process. "Now should the shavings be light or dark?" he loudly asks over the drill.

"Light!" the entire class yells, still covering their ears.

"Miss Meadow taught you well," he comments, removing the drill from the tree. Just as the students answered, a pile of beige wood shavings pop out of the tree like a firework exploding in the sky. "Now I need you to help me put the tap in."

"Make one line," Miss Meadow instructs, guiding the students into an orderly fashion. The students stretch their necks over the line, their colorful heads from the hats wave like flowers in a field as they shift to get a view of the tree. The tree worker slides the spout into the loose bark.

"One hit each," he informs, handing over a hammer to the first student in line. As instructed, each student gives the spout one single hit, tapping the metal drain pipe deeper into the bark. Stevey approaches the tree. He gives the spout a good hit, hands the hammer to the classmate behind him, and runs over to me. He holds onto his big, floppy hat as he reaches my side.

"Did you see that?" Stevey gleams, pulling on my arm.

"Nice job Stevey," I reply. Stevey smiles, looking up to me.

"Thanks for the green hat," he says.

"You're welcome," I smile. "Is green your favorite color?"

"No," he shakes his head. "You had a green hat and I wanted to match with you." Sliding his hand down my arm, he reaches for my hand. Surprised, I lower my gaze as his tiny palm rests in mine. "This is so much fun! I can't wait to tell JJ!" My heart melts as we continue to hold hands. Not letting go, we stay in this moment, holding hands with our matching green hats.

***

After Stevey's class completed their lesson, Cali and I continued working. My body acted as a pendulum, moving back and forth between the tree workers and the work stations. The day was more strenuous on my legs, especially with the sun beating down on us. With my shaved head, I am thankful to be wearing some sort of protection on my almost naked scalp.

The next day was our last trade run item: honey. Just as Stevey did yesterday with tree tapping, I got to assist in the process of honey collection. Gearing up in the full protective suit was intimidating at first, but once I was surrounded by the bees, I was not scared at all. I found myself genuinely having fun and even… laughing. Joining Stevey's class and playing the role of beekeeper for a day, I experienced firsthand how much of an operation it is to run Cali. Similar to Amella's film sets, there is an enormous amount of work behind the scenes with multiple moving parts for one common goal. As I work on this special project, I find myself disagreeing with Wila's opinion on Cali's role. Yes, she keeps Cali alive, but she does that because she is in fact the leader. Wila said there is no hierarchy here but, in my eyes, there is. Without Cali, this place would not function. Without Cali, this place would not have proper organization. Without Cali, there simply would be no Cali.

My eyes open as my sore body stays curled like a shell under the warm blankets. After three days of walking, packing, organizing, and lifting, I was pleased Cali designated today as our rest day from physical labor. Sleeping in, I am not sure what time it is, but judging by the sunlight shining over the middle of our tent, I am guessing early afternoon.

Relaxing my muscles with a hot shower, I dry off and put on fresh clothes. I stare back at my reflection, still adjusting to the 'new look'. Before I think about it too much, I leave the tent and make a right. Usually, I turn left to exit the living quarters, but Cali wants to meet at her tent today. Resembling the head of a long table, I walk to the last tent located at the end of the path. I stand, debating if I should enter or not. The predicament of curtains, no way to knock on a door.

"You may enter," Cali calls from inside. Guess she knew I was here. Embarrassed, I separate the curtains and venture inside. "Sleep well?"

"Yes," I reply, taking in my surroundings.

Expecting Cali's tent to resemble everyone else's, I am taken aback by the open floor plan. Rather than specific designated areas like our tent, Cali's is one large living room. The walls on either side are masked with bookshelves. Sardined, there is no empty slot available as each book is pressed together like an accordion. Neatly organized, the back wall displays a variety of collectables. Picture frames, tools, artwork, clocks, creating a museum of history.

"Please excuse the mess," Cali says, riffling through papers on a massive wooden desk sitting in front of the bookshelf.

"Mess?" I question. "This is incredible. Where did you acquire all this?" I approach the wall of collectables, inspecting each piece closely. She places her papers down, joining my side.

"Throughout the years."

"How are they able to hang on –"

"The trailer," Cali responds before I can finish. She knocks on the fabric, a hollow metal sound echoing from the opposite side. "Such a shame to forget things of the past. Reminds me of simpler times. Happier times." She smiles, brushing her aging fingers over a painting of a girl with thin, brown hair, her hands resting across one another. I watch Cali's hand on the art. My mind flashes to Frank mentioning the same ideology before he grazed his fingers over his collaged wall. Just like Frank, the girl in this artwork is a zero. "You alright?"

"Huh?" I breathe, noticing Cali staring at me with concern. "Oh, the piece is just stunning," I utter, hoping she believes my response.

"It is," she agrees, taking one last look at it. "Apologies," she turns towards me. "Today may be boring."

"How so?" I ask as Cali begins walking back to the desk.

"We'll be cross referencing the catalogues from the last trade run and this trade run."

"That does not sound too bad," I reply, making my way to the table.

"Splendid!" Cali smiles, her doe eyes bulging with excitement. Gesturing for me to sit, I obey. Similar to the wall of collectables, this chair is exquisite. "Do you prefer to work with music?"

"What do you mean?" I question as Cali heads to the other bookshelf.

"Oh," she swings forward, giggling. "Forgive me," she turns. "Keeps slipping my mind you grew up in Amella. Music to listen to, I have a record player," she states, reaching the other bookshelf.

A record player? How?

Pushing off the detailed carved arms of my chair, I race to the other side of the room. Intrigued, I stare at the record player.

"First time seeing one?" Cali smirks, sliding a record off the shelf.

"Yeah," I look to her, mirroring her smirk. "I heard of them but did not think they were real." Bending down, I inch my face closer. "I was always so curious as to how that," pointing to the record in Cali's hand, "spins on that," pointing to the record player, "and creates sound."

"Let me show you then." Stepping back, I peek over Cali's long garments as she places the record down. Lifting the needle, the record spins like the glass plate in a microwave. Steadily, she drops the needle on the record, a low crackle filling the room. Suddenly, the crackle transforms to an orchestra of instruments. Fascinated, I remain still, my ears filling with the melody. "You can pick the next record." I follow Cali back to the desk, a smile still plastered on my face.

The record player keeps us company as we work the rest of the day. The work is mundane, but it is nothing I am not used to. Similar to the Film Industry, instead of analyzing spreadsheets, I am analyzing supply information. As the moon replaces the sun in the sky, Cali illuminates the room with antique lamps throughout. The ambiance sends me back to Fred and Frank's cabin, a light warmth and glow surrounding us. Not to mention, the tent crowded from floor to ceiling with crap; déjà vu strikes at every corner.

As promised, I was able to pick the next record. Only hearing music in the six ballroom during Counting Day, I have no idea who these artists are on the covers. According to Amella standards, music creates an emotional response. No music, no books, no entertainment that can trigger negative emotions. However, I do not believe listening to music causes harmful influence. Hearing these records as I work, allowing the sweet melody to engulf my ears, it is a joyous experience. There is so much I have experienced within this short time here that Amella could never offer. For the first time, my mind is relaxing. No thoughts of guilt, regret, or boredom.

***

With the bright moon overhead, I conclude cataloging with Cali. A few tents over from ours, I hear myself humming the music that filled my ears for hours. My head bops back and forth as I fling our tent curtain open.

"Do you know what time it is young lady," Jejune jokes.

"No actually," I reply, ceasing my humming. Slipping my shoes off, I rub my tired eyes. Jejune presents the chip bag in her hand and I join her on the couch. "Stevey sleeping?" I ask, grabbing a few thin potatoes.

"Yup, he's been burning so much energy lately," she laughs. "Thanks for giving Stevey a green hat the other day, he would *not* shut up about it. It made his whole day." Jejune shoves a handful of chips in her mouth, her equally exhausted eyes staring forward. If there were any bags under either of our eyes, our dark makeup is doing a fine job covering them. "Get this," she scoffs, turning her attention to me. "I tried to *pay points* with my wrist earlier getting new overalls." Stunned, I raise my eyebrows. "I know," she confesses. "Crazy right."

"Yeah." Truthfully though, she is not crazy at all. Lowering my eyes, I think about the times I have thought of everything I used to do daily. Weigh stations, points, curfew; our routine has begun to fracture. Slowly, but not completely, like a small knick in glass leisurely expanding just before shattering the entire piece. "Do you miss Amella?" I quietly ask, almost a whisper. I shift my eyes up, reverting my gaze to Jejune. Not responding, the petals on her floral crown tremble as she munches on more chips.

"No," she states. "Have everything I need right here with me." She smiles, looking towards the hallway where Stevey is sleeping. "Didn't leave anything behind." A blow of emotion slaps me in the face.

Jejune may have everything she needs here, but I do not. I still left parts of my life behind. I left my parents who have done nothing but be great role models. I left a promising career. I left Chard who, besides Jejune, was my only true friend. A friend I did not even get the chance to say a proper goodbye to. A friend I left helpless, unable to apologize to for stolen points; he was undeserving of that. Swallowing, I gulp down the sadness as I reflect on my life before Cali, like reminiscing on a distant memory.

"Back to the grind tomorrow," Jejune exhales, placing the chip bag on the end table. Her subtle movement on the couch brings me back to reality, terminating the feelings creeping in my mind.

"JJ," Stevey mumbles, peeking through the doorframe.

"Hey little man," Jejune says sitting up. "Why are you awake?"

"Bad dream," he peeps.

"Come here." Jejune bends forward with her arms out. Rubbing his eyes, Stevey joins us on the couch, crawling onto Jejune's lap.

"Can I sleep with you tonight," he quietly pleads, nestling his head deeper into Jejune's chest.

"Of course." She brushes his hair out of his face. "No matter the time, no matter the day, I will always have my big sister JJ." Whining, Stevey wraps his skinny arms around Jejune's neck. "Come on," she groans, hoisting him on her hip as she stands. "Goodnight Rose," she whispers over her shoulder.

"Goodnight," I smile, watching Jejune trail down the hallway holding Stevey in her arms. Once alone, my smile vanishes. Uneasy, I rest my elbows on my knees, allowing my fingernails to scrape through my buzzed hair. Shakily closing my eyes, I rest my palms on my temples.

What am I doing here?

Ending my great day, I am now questioning everything. Pressure builds in my eyes as Jejune's response pulsates through my head. *'Didn't leave anything behind.'*

Although Jejune and I journeyed here together, we are now on independent wavelengths. At the end of her journey, she found a destination. At the end of my journey, I thought I found the same. I thought I did not need Amella after today, but I was only fooling myself. Jejune and I traveled here to see what this mysterious piece of land was, and we found it. We accomplished the goal, so why do we need to stay? So what if there is no curfew. So what if we can eat whatever we want. So what if there is music to listen to. Those are materialistic things that will fade and end up on Cali's wall of history one day. But my home, my true home, is with my family. That will also fade, and I cannot hang that up on a wall. Once a person is gone, they are gone. My hands remain on my head as my heart rapidly beats. I told myself I was no longer Rose Pharl the six with short brown hair who works in the Film Industry, but that Rose was safe and had stability. Right now, I want to be that Rose again. I have to go back. I have to go back to my home.

CALI

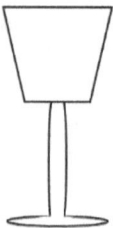

The cataloging continues. Unlike yesterday, the music filling my ears does not ease my mind. I work slower as I fight with my head. It is hard to focus on a task when your thoughts are overwhelmingly distracting. I feel as though I am trapped in the middle of an ocean during a storm. Every time I come up for air, I am slapped in the face with a new wave, struggling to breathe as water drowns my lungs. As the pencil in my hand marks the paper below me, I sneak a glance towards Cali. Our eyes meet as she watches me, her dark stare ghostly as the low lights gleam.

"Let's take a break," she states, getting up from her chair. "Come."

Vanishing through an opening between the bookshelf and the wall of collectables, I follow Cali. Now in a new room, she walks through one more opening to an enormous kitchen; Cali's tent is even larger than I thought. As my shoes go from carpet to hardwood, I realize we are now outside, a perimeter of lanterns outlining a grand porch overlooking the mountains.

"What's your poison?" Cali asks, standing at a cart filled with drinks.

"Not much of a drinker," I reply, looking back out to the mountains.

"How about a rosé for Rose?" Cali smiles, pouring me a drink. Grabbing my glass from Cali, we walk to a comfy sectional littered with pillows and blankets. We both settle into either side of the couch.

"May I?" I ask, pulling on a blanket behind me.

"Of course." Although warm from the countless lanterns, I cover my legs with the blanket as the night breeze stings my skin.

"This is beautiful," I comment, looking out to the twilight mountains.

"Favorite way to end the day," Cali remarks. "A good drink in my hand and a gorgeous view." As the soft whispers of nature blow in the wind, our conversation goes quiet. I continue to sip my refreshing, fruity drink. "Can I ask you something." Nodding, I remove the glass from my lips as Cali places hers on the table in front of us. As she leans back into the couch, her beaded necklaces chime. "Are you okay?"

"Yes," I reply back confused.

"I don't mean to be forward," she reassures. "You seem down lately."

"Yeah," I admit. "Just been a lot." Joining me, Cali grabs the blanket beside her, wrapping herself in the wool fabric. She snuggles into the couch, resting her head on the cushions. It is odd to see her in such a relaxed state.

"Your reality is distorted right now, isn't it?" I stare at Cali, her large eyes looking through me. Her floral crown shifts with the low wind, her orange hair complimenting the lanterns throughout.

"Exactly." Perfectly put, she hit the nail on the head. Leaning forward, I place my glass on the table. Allowing the couch to provide a source of comfort, I too sink into the cushions. "Just feel like I have sacrificed a lot."

"You feel guilty?" Cali inquires, raising her thin eyebrows. I flick my gaze down, debating if I should open up. Looking back to Cali, her eyes are laser focused on me. I turn my face, scanning the landscape.

"I feel like I am sacrificing time away from my family, work, home. All for what. For this?" I say, studying the high trees and skyline before me.

"Well, this isn't so bad," Cali cheerfully replies. "You know," she continues, turning my attention back to her. "When you all stumbled here two weeks ago, Jejune was the guarded one and you were more open. It seems you two have switched.

Now Jejune is more open and you're the guarded one." I stare at Cali mystified. It is as though she is reading my mind, stating aloud the dark rain cloud that has been swirling over me. "Not saying that's a bad thing," reaching across for her drink. "Just an observation."

"Your observation would be correct," I confess. I have been more guarded, but I do not want Cali to think I am guarded from her. She gave me this special project to gain trust. We have made great progress on our relationship. I hope my honest feelings I just admitted do not tarnish that.

"I was your age once. I'm surprised I made it to the age I am." A small laugh escapes her mouth. "I used to put other's needs first, always follow the rules, but then I met a little guy named time. Time is evil. You forget it exists and you blink and then years have passed." Cali stares into my eyes. "I can tell you have emotions weighing heavily on you. It's exhausting, takes a toll on you mentally and physically. It's an awful thing what our own minds can do." Numb, I continue to listen to Cali's monologue.

"Our mind feeds off our fear, it's like oxygen to it. That's why I'm here." She looks around us. "I'm here so when my mind gets the best of me, my other senses can ground me. My eyes, to take in the beauty. My ears, to listen to the tranquility. My body, to feel what's around me because if I don't, my mind will consume me." Our darkened eyes meet as I clench my blanket. "Does that make sense?"

As my throat tightens with emotion, I nervously bite my lip. I think this is the most I have ever related to anything. As pressure swells behind my eyes, I stay composed. Cali says nothing, her own eyes glimmering.

"I'm sorry," I whisper, on the brink of tears.

"Never apologize for how you feel." I nod, hearing her words but not understanding them. The encouragement to cry is so foreign, yet it feels so natural. Cali is supportive of displaying emotions, such an opposite of Amella. "Everyone has something that eats at them. The key is to not let it define you. So, what is it."

"What is what?" I ask, sucking up my emotions with a sniffle.

"What's the something that's been bugging you."

To say something is bugging me would not do my mind justice; I cannot limit it to just one thing. It is everything. Amella, my parents, the dead actress, the dead crew members, Jejune and I's relationship, the running, and running, and running. Once your mind starts, it is hard to stop. It becomes an avalanche of emotion, reflection, and self judgment. Loosening my grip on the blanket, I answer.

"Purpose," I simply state. "What is my purpose."

"Here or in the grand scheme of things?"

"Both," I shrug.

"You want my opinion." Once again, Cali leans forward, placing her now empty glass on the table. "Let that go." She collapses back, a seriousness washing over her. "Nothing matters Rose, yet, we believe everything matters. Us right here," she opens her blanket, the draped fabric making her arms look like wings of a bat, "sharing a drink with beautiful views, it won't matter. Grim, I know, but it won't. So for you to spend time searching for your purpose," she emphasizes with air quotes. "Well, it's a waste of time because if, and that's a *big* if, you do finally find your purpose, that little guy named time will have taken everything else from you to get there."

Ceasing her rant, Cali tightly wraps herself back up. Her harsh face lingers, her neck tensing as she glares at the mountains. Somehow, my 'something' has gotten her all worked up. Curious, I pry a little bit more.

"And you?"

"And me what?" she spits out. There is a change in her tone, her softness exchanged for frustration.

"What's your something," I cautiously ask. Cali exhales as my heartbeat pounds in my ears.

"I had a something, but I've moved on. Haven't wasted any time on it." A small smile creeps across her cheek. "Vanish your spheres, welcome your tears. Do you know why we wear this makeup Rose." I remain silent as her smile grows. "Autonomy. To display a total sense of independence. To prove we do not need our identity to be defined by someone else." Seeing I struck a nerve, I grab my drink, thinking of how to move on from the current conversation topic.

"Listen," Cali continues, her smile shrinking, but still present. "You're not happy here. If you want to go, you can go. I can't stop you, but Rose, if you go back, will that really change anything." I pause my drinking, processing her words. "Will you find this purpose you're searching for, or will you be trapped in the same old routine. You lived in Amella your whole life and never found your purpose then, what makes you so sure you'll find it there now." Lowering the glass from my lips, I contemplate how to reply.

"I'll think about it," I simply say.

"Please do." Her eyes crinkle as she smiles. "Well, no work tomorrow, we have the day off." Cali stands, carefully folding the blanket back on the couch, smoothing out the wrinkles. "You're welcome to enjoy the views, help yourself," she gestures to the bar. "Stay as long as you would like. To get back, follow the stairs they'll bring you to the path. I'm glad we had this talk. I can feel we are building trust." I grin as Cali stands over me. "I hope to see you at the ceremony tomorrow. Goodnight Rose."

"Goodnight." I watch Cali leave. "Thank you," I quickly shout. "Thank you for this." Not responding, Cali continues on, disappearing into her tent.

"Rose!"

"Hey Stevey," I smile as he rushes towards me.

"Close your eyes," he instructs. Doing so, I close my eyes and wait. "Open!" Looking down, Stevey is holding out a floral crown. "Now you can have a crown like everyone else!"

"Stevey..." Not expecting this at all, I am overcome with happiness as I kneel down, reaching for the crown. "You made this?" He nods.

"I wanted roses for your name but Forest didn't have any, but he gave me sunflowers." Stevey smiles. "Forest said they show friendship, and you're my friend." I touch the delicate yellow petals and look to Stevey. "I have this too!" he squeals, throwing an envelope in my face. "It's an invitation to my birthday party next week. Will you come?"

"Of course I will." His green eyes light up under his thick glasses.

"Yay!" he cheers, wrapping his arms around me. Resuming his invites, Stevey runs away, passing out envelopes to everyone at the ceremony.

"You can RSVP to me," Jejune smirks. "Stevey is making me keep a tight list, seeing as he invited the entire population of Cali."

"I am sure no one will refuse."

"No," she laughs, raising her eyebrows. "Fashionista over here," Jejune remarks as I place my crown over my head. "Twins," she states, nudging my shoulder. We both smile, our floral crowns dimly shown in the firelight.

"JJ!" Stevey sings, running back to where we are standing. "Everyone said they'll come to my birthday party!"

"That's great little man," Jejune smiles, rubbing his blonde hair.

"River said he's gonna make me a chocolate cake!"

"I hope you said thank you," Jejune states, raising her eyebrows. Stevey nods as he jitters with excitement. Grabbing his hand, they make their way to an open bench and I follow as we wait for the ceremony to start. As we sit, I scan the circle, realizing all the children are present. Last ceremony the children were not allowed to attend, I wonder what tonight's topic will be. Cali enters the circle and we all stand, acknowledging her presence.

"Welcome to our ceremony. The circle of crying ceremony." We sit back down, the fire popping loudly as Cali walks, not saying a word. Theatrics turned back on, the Cali I had a heart to heart with last night has disappeared. "We're going to try something new tonight." In the shadows of the fire, others turn to one another, confused and curious. "The universe is swirling with negativity. Good things happen, but we tend to never hear about them. So, let's hear about them!" Cali projects, raising her arms up. "Tonight, our challenge is love. Who do you love? Who loves you? What does it mean to have and give love. Finally, does love give you a sense of purpose." Cali meets my eyeline as that last word echoes in the warm air.

"I'll go," Stevey gleams, raising his hand.

"Stevey –"

"I want to," he says, cutting off Jejune's words. Hesitant, Jejune slowly slips her arms off Stevey as he scoots down from her lap. Stepping forward, Stevey adjusts his glasses. "I always feel love from my big sister, JJ. And she brought me here, where I can make friends. I miss my best friend Charlie but I have new ones. JJ is the best!" Turning around, he barrels into Jejune, squeezing her tight with a tiny hug. As the circle claps, Jejune holds Stevey close, kissing him on the forehead.

"What an incredible young boy your parents have raised," Cali remarks as the circle grows quiet.

"No," Stevey blurts. He stands next to Jejune, holding her hand. "JJ raised me. We have a saying." He turns to Jejune, reciting it directly to her. "No matter the time, no matter the day, I will always have my big sister JJ." Stevey smiles as Jejune's face becomes serious. "S.A.C.R.I.F.I.C.E." Stevey shouts over the fire. "My old teacher Mrs. Elle taught us the word sacrifice." Guilt punches me as I hear my mom's name. "Which means to stop doing something you want for someone else." A thin layer of water coats my eyes. "That's JJ. She's sacrificed a lot in her life for me. I have the best life because of her and that's why I love her."

As the circle erupts with joyous applause, Jejune tugs at Stevey, making him collapse into her arms. I look to Jejune as tears silently fall down her face, her hat covering her emotional eyes. Swelling with my own emotions, I scan the joyous crowd. Clapping, smiling, shedding tears of their own. My eyes reach Wila, Forest, and Ivy on the opposite side of the fire. Watching their family unit through the haze of the heat, Ivy rests her head on Forest. Guilt punches me once again, this time with more force. What I would give. What I would give to be able to rest my head on my dad's shoulder right now.

"Summer of love!" Cali proclaims, joining in on the celebration.

Not able to take it anymore, the thin layer of water resting on top of my eyes transforms into a gushing waterfall. Springing from my seat, I leave the ceremony, marching towards our tent. With each step, my breathing increases rapidly, the pounding throughout my head muting the dirt scraping under my feet. Fumbling to open the tent curtain, I sprint to the counter, gripping the island tightly, crushing Stevey's invitation in my hand. Heaving over, water continues to leak on my face as I desperately inhale for air.

"Rose!" I hear behind me. "Rose, what's wrong?" Through blurry vision, I see Jejune as she rubs my back, searching my face for an answer.

"I-I," I pant. "I can't."

"Can't what?" she frantically asks.

"Rose?" Stevey trembles. "Did I make you upset?"

"No baby," Jejune lovingly reassures, lifting her hand off me and rushing to his side. "Um, go change and brush your teeth, okay?" Closing my mouth, I breathe through my nose, attempting to lower my outburst. As Stevey makes his way to the bathroom, my swollen eyes see his concerned face as he clenches his clothes. "Go on baby," she instructs. Waiting until he is gone, I listen for the bathroom door to shut.

"Jejune," I whimper. "I can't stay here anymore." She places her hand on my back again as I remain hunched over.

"What?"

"I-I-" Struggling to speak, compression chokes my lungs as my torso curls in on itself. My body battles between my ice bones quivering and my swarming hot forehead.

Am I having a panic attack?

"Sit, sit, sit," Jejune calmly says. Guiding me to the couch, my hands tremble as my tense body sinks into the cushions. Tugging at my shirt, I force my neckline to my eyes, muffling my cries and soaking in my tears. "Here." I pop my head out of my shirt like a turtle. Jejune sits next to me, holding a cup of water to my lips. My exhausted face steadies as I gulp down as much water as I can. Finished, Jejune takes the cup as I close my eyes, my damp cheeks growing cold.

"I can't stay here," I breathe.

"What do you mean?"

"I have been contemplating it for a while and," I stop, opening my eyes. "I need to go home." Looking to Jejune, her lime green eyes worriedly stare.

"Home? Like back to Amella?"

"Yes. I can't take it here. I have no purpose." My voice shakes as I begin to sob. "Every day I wake up and think it will get better but then it doesn't. It gets worse and then Stevey said Elle and I thought of my mom and Ivy had her head on her dad and I thought about how much I miss my —"

Jejune embraces me, stopping my rant. Accepting her comfort, I weakly wrap my arms around her, my cries bouncing my head on her shoulder. Cali was right. Time is evil.

"Okay," Jejune whispers, continuing to hold me. "I understand." I shake my head, squeezing my eyes so tight they feel like they will never reopen. "If you want to go, you can go." Jejune releases from our embrace, lowering her head to find my saddened gaze. "But please, *please* wait until after Stevey's birthday," she begs. "It will break his heart if you aren't here. I couldn't take the look on his face when I told him Charlie wouldn't make it. Can you please stay until then?"

"Yes," I reply without hesitation. I sniffle as more tears fly off my face. For Stevey, I can stay a little longer. He is innocent in all this. I would never let my own drama affect him. I have to be strong. I was a six my whole life. Never once did I shed a tear or breakdown. I can switch back to that mindset. I was strong for twenty one years. I can be strong for one more week.

CALI

After surviving my first panic attack, I am grateful I had Jejune by my side. Even though we have had our differences lately, she was there for me. She knew exactly what to do. I do not know if I would have been able to do the same if the situation were reversed.

"You gonna be okay?" Jejune questions, packing her bag.

"Yeah, I will be alright," I say, joining her in the kitchen.

"At least your role occupies your mind," Jejune states. "No constant silence surrounded by water." That is a plus. "And don't worry," she adds, zipping up her bag. "Stevey already forgot about last night."

"That's reassuring," I laugh. "I thought I may have scared him."

"Nah, kids move on really fast." Jejune swings her bag on her shoulder. "You got time? Wanna get some breakfast?"

"I would love that," I smile. Throwing my floral crown on my head, I join Jejune down the sandy path. Who would have thought it would take having a mental breakdown to finally have a meal with my best friend again.

***

Cali has not mentioned my abrupt exit from the ceremony last night, and as we continue to work, I am fairly confident she will not bring it up. Although I am still wary about the dark makeup under my eyes, I am glad to be wearing some right now. It helps that my spheres are hidden, considering I keep losing them so quickly.

With organization and cataloging complete, our next task is packing. We leave for the trade run in four days and Cali wants to make sure we have everything prepared in time. We spend the entire day hauling each supply crate into the trailers behind the living quarters. Who knew the large, rectangular shiny homes served as more than a barrier for Cali. Limping from the weight of the crate in my arms, I slowly follow Cali as she also struggles.

"Apologies," Cali exhales, dropping her crate on the ground. "Need a minute." I give my arms relief as I too place my crate down.

"I can see why we need three days to move supplies," I joke, rolling out my shoulders.

"Usually it's a week." Cali shakily inhales through her nose.

"A week?"

"Typically, our trade run is triple this, but with the changing of seasons, we get a break each quarter."

"Guess I got the role at the perfect time," I smirk.

"Indeed." Enjoying the breeze, Cali and I silently stand. Relaxing my shoulder muscles, I squint at the trailers encircling Cali.

"Does that mean all these trailers are used for the trade run?"

"Yes. They're the perfect environment for storing supplies before they move to the truck."

"But no one lives in them?" I ask, furrowing my brow. Although the tents in the living quarters are great, the trailers could serve a better purpose than supply storage. They are trailer homes after all.

"No, our tents work just fine," Cali smiles, looking towards me. "No one goes in the trailers either. Merely for supplies." Leaning forward, Cali's beaded necklaces clank as she picks her crate back up. "Special project access only." Cali continues on, her wavy hair swinging with each step. Preparing myself, I exhale, positioning my fingers firmly under the crate before lifting.

Trudging along, we round the corner of the trailer closest to us. Same routine as the last trailer we packed, we place our crates down in front of the door as Cali finagles to get the stairs out. Finally freeing the latch, she pulls as the metal accordions out, providing steps to reach the raised door.

"Just like before," Cali instructs, walking up the steps. Following orders, I pass Cali a crate as she makes her way inside. Not letting the heat of the day enter, Cali firmly closes the door. Unaware to me, I did not know honey and syrup needed to reside in certain temperatures and dark spaces.

As Cali prepares the crate inside, I prepare the crate outside. Carefully, I hoist myself up the stairs. Not wanting to hold the weight of the crate, I prop one leg up a step, resting the crate on my knee.

SLAM!

Jumping slightly, I snap my head to the source of the loud noise. My eyes lock on the trailer next door to see Forest emerging. Confused, I watch as he jingles a set of keys, searching for the correct one. After a few attempts, he finally slides a key in the trailer door and pulls, confirming it is secure. What is he doing here? Silent, I debate if I should say anything. Before I can, he races down the steps and heads back towards the living quarters.

Not paying attention, Cali swings the door open and the hard metal collides with my knee. Losing balance, the crate topples out of my hands, crashing to the ground. Instantly, syrup seeps over the dirt. Shock sprints up my spine as I step back from the mess I made.

"I am so sorry!" I shout, running down the stairs.

"Leave it!" she states, closing the trailer door. "It's glass, don't pick it up."

"Cali I am so sorry. I —"

"Are you hurt?" she worriedly asks, looking me up and down.

"No." I look past her shoulder at the destroyed jars. "The syrup –"

"It's fine," she replies, cutting me off. "We have some left over tapped from last week. It won't take long to boil and prepare a new batch."

"I can help," I stress. "With the batch."

"Not necessary, but thank you." Cali smiles before turning back to the mess I made. "Well, let's continue on, shall we?"

"What about this?" I ask, gesturing to the puddle of thick syrup.

"Leave it for nature," Cali sings, heading back to the work stations.

Defeated, I stare at the broken glass thrown about. Before following Cali, I look up at the adjacent trailer to where Forest was, the stairs left out, evidence some-one was there. What was Forest doing in one of the supply trailers? And why would he need to lock the trailer he was in with a key?

The second day of packing the trailers, I was on high alert. My ears picked up the scraping of metal stairs opening, the labored breathing of Cali and I, but no sound of keys rattling against each other. After moving supplies and mingling at communal dinner, I aggressively rub my eyes as I get ready to shower. My eyes were exhausted from bouncing around all day searching for Forest. Washing the dried, tacky sweat off my body, I crawl into bed and instantly fall asleep.

If I had any dreams, I do not recall them as I awake from my slumber. Today is the last day of packing, or as Cali calls it, truck day. Yawn escaping my mouth, the sunburn layered upon my face painfully stretches. Learning my lesson the hard way, I swing by the sewing station to grab a hat. Mimicking Jejune's attire, I place the crown Stevey made me over my hat. As I emerge from the tent, Forest strolls past me. My feet freeze as my eyes stay locked on the shiny keys gripped firmly in his hand. Now is my chance.

Heart racing, I quiet my footsteps, stalking close behind. Making his way in between the work station tents, he slides the keys in his pocket. I begin jogging, catching up as he rounds a corner.

"Truck day!" Halting my movement, Cali steps in front of me, blocking my path towards Forest. "I brought you a hat but I see you beat me to it."

"Thanks." I peek over her shoulder to see no one. Mission failed.

"Now I won't lie to you," Cali says, making her way to the living quarters. "Truck day is not an easy day. It's my favorite, but it's a very labor intensive day."

I scan over the area one last time for Forest before joining her towards the trailers. "Are you okay with that?"

"Okay with what?" I question, finally focusing on our conversation.

"A very labor intensive day."

"After the past three days of exercise, my body should be prepared."

"Splendid. Most of the day we'll be in shade. You can give your skin a well needed break." She slightly giggles, turning away from my red flushed face. Arriving at the trailers, I look out towards the crimson mountains but my view is blocked.

"This must be the truck," I state, staring at the bulky vehicle.

"Have you ever driven a truck?"

"No, at least, not one this size." I have not seen a motor vehicle in weeks; no one uses cars in Cali. Where did this truck come from?

"Sixteen footers are hard on turns and hills, but you'll be able handle the straight paths." Cali smiles, her dark eyes glistening off the morning sun.

"You want *me* to drive that," I question, raising my eyebrows.

"Of course," she replies nonchalantly. "But not today, today we pack." I inspect the vehicle further as Cali heads to the back of the truck. There is no way Cali expects me to drive this. I have no prior experience on driving a truck full of supplies. Not even supplies, breakable, bartering supplies. Knocking me back to reality, the swoosh of the roll up door jolts me out of my racing thoughts. "Truck day!" Cali beams, her hair and garments flapping in the wind. "Let's get started, shall we?"

***

In the two and a half weeks I have been here, I now understand why truck day is Cali's favorite day. Whether it is the circle ceremony speeches, the repetitive daily schedule, or the borderline obsessive trade run organization, Cali exhibits one trait: order. Everything needs to be in order. Nothing can be at fault. No flaws. No mishaps. For truck day, she is positively jittery with the arrangement of the truck. I cannot lie, Cali may be a complete perfectionist, but the presentation of the truck's interior is magnificent.

"Rose, you can cross reference now."

Climbing up the loading ramp, I flip to this trade run's checklist. I stand before all the supplies, meticulously reading each item as I count the stacked crates.

20 crates of bamboo: check.

20 crates of syrup: check.

20 crates of honey: check.

30 coolers: check.

5 oak slabs

Oak slabs? Confused, I study the supplies closely, reconfirming there are only crates and coolers.

"Hey Cali," I call over my shoulder. Checking the sheet again, I wait as her footsteps crunch towards me. "Do we have five oak slabs?" I look up from the checklist, turning to see Cali standing before me.

"Oh dear. It slipped my mind." She sighs, her tired eyes sinking like the sun setting around us. "Could you check with the woodworkers if the slabs are ready."

"Sure." Placing the clipboard down, I hop off the truck. Walking up and down the loading ramp all day, my knees are screaming in agony as I make my way to the woodworking station. I sure will sleep like a rock tonight. Engulfing my ears, screeching saws greet me as I finally reach the woodworking station. Unsure who to talk to, I find a worker sitting on a stool slowly shaving a spoon.

"Hi Rose," the man says, placing his spoon and tools down.

"Hi," I reply, embarrassed to not know his name. "Cali sent me here to see if the oak slabs were ready?"

"This way," he shouts over the buzzing. Leaving the loudness, my nostrils swarm with the smell of sawdust as we head into an adjacent tent. "Pete!" Halting his sanding, Pete looks up and removes his face covering.

"What'd you need?" he asks, resting his sawdust powdered arms on his hips.

"Does five oak slabs ring a bell," the other worker asks.

"Sure does," Pete smirks, knocking on the wood below him. "Aye!" he calls. "How are the other four coming along?" Turning my head, I look to the other workers, their hands scraping sandpaper back and forth. "Give us another hour or so." I nod, making my way back out of the tent.

"Hey Pete!" one of the workers shouts. "It might only be four slabs."

"Hold on," Pete states, stopping my movement. "What's wrong?" he asks, walking over to the other workers.

"You ever seen this before?" the worker asks, stepping back from the slab. As if the slab is a magnet, all the surrounding workers huddle together, inspecting the piece of wood. Keeping his focus locked on the wood, Pete raises his arm, waving over the worker who led me here.

"Come look at this." Curious, I join the crowd of workers. "What's that look like to you?" I look to where his finger is pointing. Ruining the sleekness of the wood, an embedded small, silver circle shines.

"A coin?" a young worker questions.

"Fisher, did you get a drill bit stuck in there again," one worker scoffs.

"I wasn't even working on this slab!" Fisher defends.

"It's none of those," Pete states, shushing the bickering. "You know what that looks like." I stare at Pete, eagerly awaiting his thought. "A bullet."

A bullet?

"What are you on Pete," a worker hollers, aggressively rubbing shavings off his thick arm hair. "That couldn't be a –"

"Keep your voice down," another worker snaps. Anxious, I keep quiet, continuing to eavesdrop on the conversation.

"How's that possible," Fisher says.

"What do you mean how's that possible," Pete echoes, standing upright. "How it's possible means someone shot it."

"Shot it with what?" Fisher asks, looking around the huddle.

"What do you think Fisher," Pete scoffs. "Someone shot it with a gun."

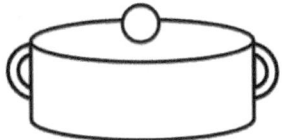

"A gun?" Fisher laughs. "That's not possible."

"Do you know how guns work?" the worker next to him asks.

"I'm not that dumb," Fisher exclaims. "I'm saying it's not possible because who would've shot it?" No one responds. "We don't have guns here." Heart beating, I silently agree. Fisher is right, Cali said no weapons allowed.

"Thank you captain obvious," Pete huffs. "You may know how guns work, but this bullet could be from decades ago."

"It can't be," Fisher states. "Look at the callus." Knowing nothing about woodworking, I study the slab, dissecting Fisher's insight. "That's where the tree started healing itself. It's like the scab from the damage. The callus isn't even complete meaning it's gotta be fairly recent."

"Fisher's right," a worker adds. "Tree's got lighter bark too. Hasn't aged that much."

"Thank you," Fisher smiles, nodding to everyone else.

"No way," a worker scoffs. "If there was a gun we'd have heard it."

"I'm not saying it happened yesterday," Fisher defends. "But probably in the last couple years."

"Since when do you know so much about a tree's healing process," another worker adds. "I'm surprised callus is even in Fisher's vocabulary." All the workers laugh as Fisher's face frowns with anger. Erupting with opinions, all the workers start speaking over one another.

My eyes stay glued to the bullet lodged in the wood. Matching the sunburn on my face, my cheeks become hot with panic. If all that is true and the tree is new, that means the bullet is new. The only citizens in Cali I know that would have a gun are myself and Jejune. Could it have been Jejune? No, that worker is right, someone would have heard a gun go off. Cali is a small place, a sound like that would echo all throughout. So then how did it get there? When and who would have –

"Enough gentlemen," Pete sighs. A silence falls through the tent as the workers stop their ranting. "Sorry these hooligans kept you waiting," he states, looking to me. "Let Cali know we have four slabs ready. If she's got a problem with that, she can come and see the fifth herself." Calming my anxiety, I politely smile, making my exit out of the tent. "Also," Pete commands. "I shouldn't have to say this, but this stays here." The workers firmly nod as they resume their tasks. Doing the same, I nod towards Pete as I hold the tent curtain open. Dropping the fabric, I venture back to the truck.

What the fuck is going on?

Mysterious bullets. Mysterious keys. The mysteries continue to swirl around me like a tornado forming. The winds are slow at first, but once gaining momentum, the hurricane is unstoppable. That is how my mind feels, my questions and confusion persistently building. Frustrated, I march past the trailers, the flaps of my hat bouncing with each stride.

"How are the slabs?" Cali smiles, popping her head out of the truck. I need to calm down. I need to confront Cali about all the recent events, but not yet. I need to make sure I have all my facts straight.

"They only have four ready," I state. "They have a problem with the fifth. Pete said if you want you can look at it."

"I'll take a look." Cali walks down the ramp. "That was the last item on our list and the sun is setting," she looks to the dimly lit sky. "Let's call it a night."

"Sounds good. What time do we leave tomorrow?"

"Early," Cali states wide eyed. "Before the sun even rises."

"Oh," I respond, raising my eyebrows. "How early?"

"The magic hour. Which you should be no stranger to."

"Yup." I used to wake up before the magic hour constantly for filming. Now I sleep in until much after sunrise. My body has gotten so accustom to Cali time, but I can manage reverting back to Amella time for one morning.

"Sleep well," Cali smiles as we walk our separate ways. Exhausted, I take my floral crown and hat off, rubbing my skull. My hair is beginning to grow back, the tough prickliness slowly being replaced by soft centimeters of hair. I smile to myself. Following the lit lanterns, a smell wafts from our tent, my nose sniffing something brewing in the kitchen as I enter.

"Hey," Jejune nods, stirring a pot on the stove.

"Cooking?" I question, sitting on an island counter stool.

"Yeah," she covers the pot. "Stevey doesn't feel good."

"Is he okay?" I ask, looking down the hallway.

"Yeah, he'll be fine. Poor guy just laid down." Jejune frowns, leaning on the counter. "Probably run down from being outside all the time. He plays every day with his friends." Jejune smiles, her eyes lighting up with joy. "He wants to get better before his birthday celebration."

"I am sure he will," I smirk, placing my hat and crown down. Jejune pushes off the counter, facing the stove again.

"Do you want any of this soup?" she asks.

"No, I do not want to eat Stevey's food."

"Doubt he'll eat this," Jejune scoffs, stirring the pot as steam wiggles out. "That boy is *very* picky." The room falls silent as she continues to cook.

"The woodworkers found a bullet in a slab today." Although Pete instructed us to keep that information a secret, I trust Jejune.

"Jeez." She turns down the heat on the stove, placing the cover on the pot. Facing me, she clasps her hands together, elbows resting on the counter.

"They think it is recent," I add, trying to read Jejune's reaction.

"Shit," she scoffs, shaking her head. "Guns are everywhere."

"Well, not everywhere." Heart beating, I look at Jejune, not knowing how she is going to react. Furrowing her brow, she stares through me.

"You think I had something to do with it?" Not responding, the dark makeup under her eyes stretches as she raises her eyebrows. "You can't be serious." I hitch my shoulders up.

"No one else has guns here and you know how to –"

"Come on Rose," Jejune stands up. "You think I'm sneaking out in the middle of the night to have target practice?" She scoffs, crossing her arms over her chest.

"The bark on the tree was young, and the workers suggested that –"

"When did you all the sudden become a tree expert," Jejune snaps, cutting me off. She is right, I cannot take their word. The bullet could be a day old or a decade old. I may not be a tree expert, but I do know trees can live for hundreds of years. I never should have brought this up.

"I'm sorry."

"You should be," Jejune states, standing stern. "You know, I was very sympathetic to your episode the other night, but obviously you do need to go back. Your head is not right."

"Lucky for you I leave for the special project tomorrow." I wait for a response as Jejune opens a cabinet. Some best friend she is being right now.

"Okay," she says, reaching for a bowl.

"Okay?" I say. "That's it?" Jejune closes the cabinet, looking to me with a bowl in her hand.

"Good luck," she shrugs. Jejune turns, filling the bowl with soup. My shoulders sink, my anger changing to sadness. The last time we were separated, Jejune confessed how nervous she was I would be playing the role of Aster. Now, only a shrug and a good luck. My Amella training prepared me for an array of situations, but not this one. Nothing can prepare you for how it feels to lose a friend. As vulnerability rises to my eyes, I ask the question to the topic that has hurt me the most.

"Why didn't you tell me."

"Tell you..." Jejune questions, searching for a spoon.

"About your scar." I blink rapidly, trying to dry my hazy eyes. "About how you got it."

"Never came up." Even if it never came up, she could have been open with me. Someone she trusts. Someone she has known for years.

"What about me?"

"What about you." Jejune throws the spoon in the bowl, slamming it on the counter. "It isn't always about you Rose. Telling that story had nothing to do with you being my friend or not."

"Then what?" I exclaim. "What did it have to do with?"

"It actually felt good to tell the truth," she replies, lowering her voice. Jejune grabs the spoon, quietly stirring the bowl on the counter. She stares at the soup, her green eyes unblinking. "To not be shunned or silenced like in Amella. The people here actually look at me and not just at my scar." Jejune lifts the spoon, tasting the soup. "I didn't cry at the ceremony because I was sad, I cried from relief. Relief I don't have to make sure I get home at a certain time or make sure I don't spend too many points." Finally making eye contact with me, she places the spoon back in the bowl. "I can wake up and know Stevey will have food and be safe. It's what he needs. It's what I need." We remain staring at one another with our dark eyes.

"I just wish you would've told me. I wouldn't have judged you."

"I'm not an idiot Rose," Jejune smirks. "I know you wouldn't have judged me. Besides, that wasn't the true story." Jejune looks to me, a seriousness washing over her face. "That's for only me to know."

"I understand," I simply reply.

"I'm glad you took on this special project. We all need a break from one another. We spent way too much time together getting here, it'll be nice to do our own things for a while." I feel like we have been doing our own things since the moment we arrived. "This is cold now." Jejune empties the bowl into the warm pot, mixing the soup thoroughly before scooping a new portion. "In all seriousness," Jejune concludes. "I do hope you have a safe trip. Stevey and I will be waiting to hear all about it when you get back." She smiles, her eyes looking to me. I return the smile as I study her dark eyes, missing the times her scar would shine.

Stevey's small voice fills the tent as Jejune brings him his warm soup. Their voices in the hallway drown out my silence in the kitchen, leaving me on an island of isolation. Our relationship is separating like a rubber band. We keep stretching further and further apart, and at some point, the band has to snap. My eyes water as I look to the floral crown Stevey made me. I do not want our rubber band to snap, leaving behind two divided parts. I want everything to be how it was a couple weeks ago. Wild how much everything can change in so little time.

The magic hour air stings my arms as I walk to the truck. My eyes take in the cotton candy colored sky rising above the deep magenta mountains. Enjoying the view, I try not to think about Jejune and I's conversation last night. I wish we would have left on better terms.

"Good morning," Cali says, waiting by the truck. "Sleep well?"

"Surprisingly good." Untying the jacket around my waist, I slip my chilled arms through. "How about you?"

"Wonderfully," she smiles, her cheekbones rising towards her dark eyes. "I hope you're ready for a long day of travel."

"Yes," I reach around to tap my backpack. "Brought snacks."

"Excellent. There's also a cooler with drinks and food for our journey." Cali grabs the handle above her, the wide truck door swinging open. "I can get us onto the main road, once it's a straight shot, you can drive if you feel comfortable." Cali hoists herself up into the truck as I walk to the passenger side. Finally leaving the cool breeze, I get settled in the truck. Buckling my seatbelt, I look over the dashboard, realizing how high up we are. Feeling eyes on me, I turn to see Cali staring at my head. "Apologies," she confesses. "I haven't seen you without a hat recently."

"Oh yeah," I laugh, touching my hair. "It is starting to grow."

"I can see, your natural color is coming back." Hunching over, I study my reflection in the side mirror, examining my dark roots as they grow like lead in a well sharpened pencil. "Let's hit the road!"

Sitting back straight, Cali starts the engine, the low rumble vibrating my seat. The bright headlights illuminate our path, disrupting the sleeping nature around us. I sneak a glance to Cali, her long sleeves hanging over the steering wheel. The contrast between Cali's vibrant, colorful garments against the gray, stagnant interior of the truck is bizarre. It is a strange sight to see Cali in such a commercialized environment. As we trek over the desert terrain, I keep my focus forward. Continuing to sightsee, I ponder what conversation topics we can have. We are going to be in this truck for eight hours. We cannot spend the entire truck ride in silence.

***

We do have sporadic conversations as the hours tick on, but nothing too deep. Thankfully, Cali brought CDs, which helped the times our dialogue stopped. As early dawn changed to morning, I drove. Having never driven a truck before, I know I was driving slower than Cali wanted. My knuckles were sore from tensely gripping the wheel as my foot cautiously stepped on the accelerator. The music helped. My body may have told a different story, but the melody did ease my mind.

Before switching, we pulled off for a bathroom break and lunch. If there is one thing I love about Cali, it is their bread. It is so fluffy and delicious. Nothing like the bread back in Amella. With the sun above serving as our clock, the hours went by faster than I thought. Magic hour, to dawn, to afternoon, to dusk, to night, the sluggish bright star took its bow as the moon claimed center stage. Cali was hoping to arrive before sundown, but my heedful driving added more time than anticipated. Nonetheless, I am glad Cali drove the night shift. The view out my window is pure darkness, I would have no idea where I was going. No lights. No cars. No presence of anyone else. Just Cali and I rolling along in a huge truck.

"Here we are." Cali peers over the windshield, taking a wide turn.

As we hug an unseen corner, the landscape drastically changes before us. Being accustom to the mountains as a constant backdrop, my eyes grow wide as the sky stretches on for miles, covered in a confetti of stars. My focus shifts down to the ground as small hills stack on top of each other. As the truck slows, I realize those are not hills I am seeing, those are waves. Suddenly, Cali turns away from the water, the headlights inches from a wall of nocturnal green trees.

"Can you guide me?"

"What?" I ask.

"Could you hop out and stand on my side." She puts the truck in reverse. "Tell me when I am close enough to the dock."

The dock? Was there a dock?

Unbuckling, I jump out of the truck, my feet sinking into soft ground. As I shut the door, I crouch, brushing my hand over the surface. A gasp escapes my mouth as my fingers tingle from the fine mineral.

Sand?

Standing up, I round the back of the truck, but this time it is my eyes that stop me. A dimly lit narrow dock rests on top of the open water. Squinting, I faintly make out a huge dark blob floating beside it.

Where are we?

"You okay, Rose?" Cali calls from the truck. Hustling, I make it to the driver side. Raising my arms, I motion for Cali to move. I keep waving, firmly shooting my palm towards her to stop. The engine shuts off, the blinding reverse lights burning out as I turn back towards the water. I remain frozen as Cali joins my side.

"Is this the ocean?"

"Yes. Have you –" Cali gently covers her mouth. "Oh, you've never seen the ocean, have you?"

"No," I mutter, continuing to stare out at the giant sea. All my senses flood with the water before me. Ears with the crashing of waves. Nose with the thickness of salt. Body with the chill of the ocean breeze. Eyes with the beauty of it all. "It is just how my mom described it." A sob builds in my throat as I hear my own words.

"Well, the vampire beach doesn't do it justice. Just wait until daytime. Did you grab your bag?" I shake my head. "Grab your bag and then we'll head inside."

Inside?

I look to the dark outline next to the dock, realizing it is a massive boat. Slowly backing away, I keep my sights on the ocean as I grab my bag. I follow Cali's dark shadow onto the dock, our steps echoing off the solid wood. My mind fills with an eeriness, our hollow footsteps bringing me back to that night on the wooden dock. Gunshots. Blood. Night crew. Dead eyes. "Have you been on a boat before?"

"Yes," I respond, coming back to reality. "But not one like this." Compared to the boat Jejune, Stevey, and I traveled in, this one makes ours look like a toy. I would not even classify this as a boat, it is a monstrous yacht.

"She is a beauty!" Reaching the boat, we step through a small opening, the dull dock bulbs providing a source of light. How on earth did Cali acquire something like this? Sensing our movement, a light flicks on above us, reflecting off a glass sliding door. "We'll unload the truck tomorrow. We can rest and sleep in, the trade run isn't scheduled until night."

Chiming over the constant waves back on the shore, I see a group of keys in Cali's hand. With the spotlight above, it does not take me long to confirm those are the same set of keys Forest had. The same mix of bronze and rusty gold metal jingling. Heart beating, my tired eyes quickly count five keys, immediately recounting each to confirm. One is to a trailer back in Cali. Another is to the door of this boat. I wonder what the other three could be for. Turning the key, Cali slides the glass door open, her darkened eyes staring at me with a smirk before she speaks.

"Welcome to your home on the water."

"Give me a minute to get the power on."

As Cali disappears into the dark boat, I make my way to the railing. The reflection of the moon dances across the water, rising and falling with each ripple. Looming at the sea, my mind floods with memories from the dock. The way my heart pumped violently through my chest I thought it would explode out. The way my rapid breathing made my lungs beg for air. The way my ear would not stop ringing. The high pitch ping steady in my ear, like a mosquito was nestled in there, buzzing right beside my eardrum. My neck hangs down, forcing me to focus on the water and relive that awful night. Gunshot. Gunshot. Heartbeat. Breathing. Ringing.

A loud hum sounds as a sapphire glow seeps from under the boat. My body relaxes as my nightmare memory fades away. Hypnotized, my eyes adjust to the blue artificial luminescence.

"Apologies," Cali states, staggering out onto the deck. "My knees and those engine room stairs are not friendly. Come on in." Entering, my eyes adjust to the bright lights shining off the glossy wood. "There was a living and kitchen area, but both were removed for storage. I'll show you the rooms." Continuing the tour, we squeeze through a tight hallway, surprisingly housing a full bathroom and two bedrooms; it is like a home on the water. "Pick whichever one you'd like."

Eyeing each bedroom, I pick the one with a small window, showing nothing but darkness outside. Walking into the room, I drop my bag at the edge of the bed.

103

My eyes stop on the blanket, noticing small embroidered flowers, more specifically roses.

"You're welcome to shower." Turning away from the bed, I look to Cali. "I'm going to head back out and connect to shore power." She gives me a small smile, her dark eyes scrunching. "Oh," she adds, turning back quickly, sending her draped clothes swinging. "If you get hungry, I'll leave the cooler down the hall."

"Thank you. Any time I should be up by?"

"No," she shakes her head. "Whenever the sun wakes you," pointing to the window above my bed. "Well, goodnight then." As the sound of Cali's beaded necklaces fade, I approach my door, sealing it shut.

Turning off the overhead lights, I click on the small nightstand lamp. As a yawn escapes my mouth, I search for my pajamas. After a long day of travel, my body warms like bread in an oven under the sheets. Laying in bed, I stare through my skylight, a few stars twinkling above. I feel the ever subtle movement of the water, but not too much. Similar to how the earth is always spinning, but we do not feel it. I always thought that was so strange as a child when my dad told me that. Another star twinkles. I miss my dad.

I click the lamp off, turning over to stare at the blank wall in front of me. This is the fourth bed I have slept in since the start of our venture. I am grateful, the hard ground in the woods was not ideal, but I want my bed back. There is just something about wrapping yourself in your own blanket, resting your head on your own pillow. A different kind of comfort.

The cozy covers brush across my chin as I curl up, allowing sleep to take hold. I will be in my own bed soon. After this it is Stevey's birthday and then I can leave. I can finally see my mom and dad again. I can finally be in the North again. I can finally sleep in my own bed again.

***

The minute rocking of the boat kept me in a deep slumber. Cali's bedroom door is shut as I emerge from the bathroom. Unsure when she will wake up, I quietly open the sliding door and walk to the front of the boat. Cali was right, the vampire beach did not do the ocean justice. Closing my eyes, I sniff like a dog searching for a treat, filling my nose with the salty air.

"The ocean is beautiful Rose. When the morning sun shines over it, all your worries go away."

My mom's voice echoes in my head. Opening my eyes, I think of her words, enjoying the serene view. My mom visited the ocean once and wished to go someday with me. If only she was here now. Some moments in life are good, but they would be great with the right person standing next to you.

"Good morning!" Peeking over my shoulder, I spot Cali approaching. "Beautiful isn't it." Just as I did, Cali inhales deeply, shakily closing her eyes. "Jungles, mountains, deserts, oceans. It's one strange rock we live on. It's magical."

"So you get to see this view every trade run."

"Yes. Some days are good, some days are bad." Her doe eyes bulge out of her dark makeup. "The ocean can be a very unforgiving terrain."

"I hope you are not expecting me to drive this boat then," I laugh, trying to lighten the mood. Knowing Cali, anything is possible.

"No," she giggles. "But you'll be my co-captain. Assisting me with the dock lines, navigation, things of that nature."

"That I can handle," I grin.

"Splendid," she sings. "No rush but I've put the loading ramp down. When you are ready, we can begin packing up the boat." Slightly trembling, Cali carefully makes her way to the edge of the deck.

Before joining, I take one last look at the water. Resembling a blue table cloth, the ocean is flat and still. The terrain does not appear to be unforgiving this morning. Overlooking the serene landscape, I am reminded I am not trapped in complete water. Surrounded by a fence of trees, I feel as though I am back in the North. Back in Amella. Back home. As the sun shines over the water, my mind is calm. The calmest it has been in a while. My mom was right, my thoughts are like a receding wave, the foamy liquid being swallowed by the sea. Vanishing in one swift motion. Day or night on this trade run, I will not be alone. I will have my mom's memories of the ocean during the day, and my dad's presence of the stars sparkling above me during the night. With that in mind, my worries are going away.

The boat ride has not been great. With each lift over the bumpy water, my stomach flips as I grip the railing. Thankfully the high speed of the boat combined with the wind is blowing my throw up away. Stomach now empty, I spit and wipe the grossness from my lips. I weakly round the back of the deck, taking the small wooden stairs up to the flybridge.

"It happens to everyone," Cali shouts over the roaring propellers. Fearful I will upchuck again, I keep my mouth closed. The hot leather sizzles my legs as I sit on the couch next to the control panel. Wind whipping my face, I rest my head back, placing my hands over my queasy stomach. "The water will be less choppy soon."

Although I am not enjoying my first yacht ride at this moment, I am glad I got sick now and not earlier. We spent the entire morning unloading the truck. Unlike carrying the crates on flat land in Cali, it was more strenuous walking the entire dock and safely getting ourselves and the supplies on the boat. I can see why Forest was the last one in this role, definitely easier with man power. Cali used her extreme organization skills to neatly store the supplies inside, even creating an opening to still be able to access the bathroom. As we prepped the boat for sailing, it was evident Cali should have picked Jejune for this special project. Between untying the dock lines, disconnecting from shore power, hoisting up the fenders, we wasted more time with Cali having to instruct me step by step. With Jejune, she would know all this boat maintenance no problem. Cali did let me use the thrusters when we were leaving the dock. I may have just been pushing a switch, but it was cool to do.

Soon enough we steadily glide across the ocean, the movement of water trailing behind like twirling ribbons. Cali's long clothes blow rapidly as the evening creeps around us. The further we travel, the trees holding me to land become scarcer. Erasing the hope of land nearby, I circle around to only see water. In the blink of an eye the clear turquoise sea darkens to murky indigo. Standing, I walk to the front, staring at the night sky above. I study the stars, searching for a constellation.

"We're heading south," I state, keeping my neck back.

"How do you know that?" Cali shouts behind me.

"The stars." Smiling, I look away from the sky, turning to Cali as the cold air stings my face. "My dad taught me." Not responding, Cali draws her attention to the control panel below her. "Do you need help navigating?"

"We're actually here…" she trails off, finagling with multiple buttons. As if a curtain opened revealing a stage, the dark landscape is replaced with scattered lights. Cali turns the boat, the dispersed lights outlining a shoreline as we draw nearer. "Could you put out the fenders and dock lines?"

Holding the railing, I carefully make my way down to the deck. Grunting, I pick up each fender, sliding it down and over the edge of the boat. Sloppily, I fumble with the bundled dock lines, tossing them over as well. Breathing deeply, I look back out to the shore, trying to make out where we are. The illuminating lights reveal a lengthy dock, rising high above the low tide and leading into darkness. The night air is deafening quiet, no sight or sound of anyone else. Breaking the silence, my eyes catch the anchor as it plummets under the water, the heavy chain barely reflecting as it rapidly unravels. Confused, I wait as Cali makes her way down the stairs.

"Let's head inside until it's time."

"No dock lines?" I ask, joining her through the sliding door.

"The anchor will hold us for now. We're early so no need to dock quite yet." Cali walks down the hall towards her room. "Give me one minute." Waiting for Cali in the tightly cramped space, she emerges with a pile of clothes in her hands. "Did you bring your floral crown?"

"No, I left it. Did I need it?"

"No that's my fault. Take these," she hands me the pile of bright fabrics, "and I'll get you a crown." I flip through the clothes as Cali leaves again. Blue ombre, bright red, green cotton. I stop searching as she returns with a crown, opal petals neatly placed all around. "You can throw a shawl over your clothes, they won't know the difference."

"Is there a reason for all this," I ask, gesturing to my outfit change.

"So you look the part. Not to be rude but," she purses her lips in thought. "You still look like you're a citizen of Amella. In Cali we wear this." Just as I did, she gestures to her garments. "We don't want any reason for eyebrows to be raised while we trade." I furrow my brow, trying to understand. "Simply pretend, go with it. Improvise if you have to." Cali smiles at me. "You know like you used to do."

"Used to do?" I ask, slipping my head through a brightly colored shawl.

"You know, as an actress." Cali approaches me, presenting the crown.

"I was never an actress."

"But," Cali stops, her arms frozen above my head. "You work in the Film Industry."

"Yes, in the Sound Department," I quickly say. "I am a boom operator." Bowing, Cali places the crown on my head.

"I see." Lifting my head, our eyes meet. We stand like this for some time, our postures mirroring one another. The faint sound of footsteps slices the tension in the air. "That's them." Cali makes her way out of the room onto the deck. Looking down, I straighten out my large shawl. "Are you coming, boom operator?"

I stop smoothing out my clothes, popping my head up at Cali. The sea breeze slaps her hair, the long orange strands draping over her face. As she steps onto the deck, the wind gives one final gust, sending the trim of her shawl flying, like leaves floating off the ground. Within that moment, my eyes fall to her hands. Goosebumps crawl on my skin as I stare at her fists. Unlike the soft swaying of her clothes, her hands are hard. Tightly clenched and knuckles white as snow.

"Cali –"

"Let me do the talking." She strikes her hand up, stopping my explanation. It is obvious she is upset. Not upset, furious. Furious that her assumptions of my occupation were incorrect. Walking past me, Cali lowers her hand and stands by the railing as the boat slowly parks next to the dock. "Oh?" Cali questions. "Hello?"

"Hey there!" a young man yells. I peer over the railing as the man briskly secures the lines to the dock. Oddly, this man does not have dark makeup or spheres under his eyes. He is a zero. "You must be Cali."

"Where's Timothy?" Cali asks, a hint of aggravation in her voice.

"I dunno," he shrugs. "Said he had to be somewhere else."

"Hmm," Cali breathes. "Did he say where?" The man frowns, shaking his head. "Alright, who am I working with then?"

"I'm Andre," the man smiles. "And my partner's coming shortly." I wish I were Andre right now. Nice long jacket, comfy cargo pants, thick boots. He looks so warm compared to the thin clothing I am wearing. I wrap the shawl around my arms, the ocean wind cutting my bare skin like sharp icicles. "Cali and, your name miss?" Frozen, my eyes flick to Cali; she told me to let her do all the talking. She stares at me, waiting for me to speak.

"Rose." Footsteps approaching, Andre turns to look down the dock.

"Ah," Andre grins, his sphereless face scrunching with joy. "New guy, introduce yourself."

"Hi," Andre's partner states, coming into the light. "I'm Charden." My heart stops immediately. Bones frozen with shock, I stare at Chard, face also sphereless, as he looks to Cali and I. My eyes flutter rapidly as I make sure I am seeing what I am seeing. Not reacting to me standing right in front of him, Chard looks to Andre.

"Would you like us to come –"

"We'll come to you gentlemen," Cali firmly states, unlatching the door, cutting Andre off.

Chard presents his hand for Cali which she ignores, stepping onto the dock without a glance his way. Utterly confused, I stare at Chard, wondering why he is not saying anything. Why he does not recognize me, then I remember, I do not look like the Rose he knows. Buzzed blonde hair, dark makeup, sunburned face, mixed with my new attire. To him, I look like a complete stranger. I place my palm in his as I step over the water, too stunned to speak.

Hypnotized, I fixate on his face with zero spheres, trying to put the puzzle pieces together. What is Chard doing here? Why does he have no spheres? In Amella, if you are a zero, you are sent away for retraining. How is he working? Realizing I am not in Amella anymore, I blink hard; Amella standards are endlessly engraved in me. But if we are not in Amella, where is the dark makeup under his eyes? Unless… are we in Amella? No, that does not make sense. Chard works in the Film Industry. Did he lose his job? I stumble as dizziness spins inside my mind.

"Woah, you alright?" Chard places his hand on my shoulder as concern fills his face. My confusion is soon replaced with terror. As Chard stands before me, I question if what is happening right now is even real.

Am I going crazy?

"Charden!"

He gives me a sympathetic smile as his hand brushes off my shoulder. I try to say something, but he has already turned away. No, I am not imagining this, Andre just said the name Charden out loud. Circling around, sickness fills my stomach as I eye the gray water. I have to figure out what is going on. Beginning my walk, I haul it to the end of the dock.

"Andre, Charden," I catch Cali say as I arrive to the shoreline. "How many do you count there." Trying my best to act normal, I calmly follow Cali's gaze, my eyes seeing ten large crates.

"Ten miss," Andre states, hands on hips.

"Charden?" Cali asks wide eyed.

"Ten," he states. I stare at Chard, an upset look across his face. The same look he had after his brother punched him in the face outside the SRC.

"There should be twenty." Cali overlooks the crates, a long silence hanging in the air. "Why are there only ten?"

"We ran out of time," Andre says.

"Ran out of time?" Cali annunciates, turning to face them both.

"Apologies Cali. With Timothy suddenly leaving the island, we ran short on time. We didn't wanna be late." I strain to focus on the conversation, but I am distracted as I attempt to analyze Chard's involvement in all this.

"I would rather you have been late with the full supply than on time with half the supply." Andre and Chard fidget, not responding.

"We understand," Andre nods. "We can come back –"

"Do you think my time is strictly allotted to wait for your screw up." Tension strikes my spine as I stand before them all. "Do you gentlemen?"

"We sincerely apologize Cali."

"Apology not accepted." Uneasy, my mind flashes to the night crew questioning Jejune, Stevey, and I, the same confrontational tone in Cali's voice. The air disguises my trembling of nerves to merely look like I am shivering from the cold.

"So which item would you also like half of?" In unison, Andre, Chard, and myself snap our heads to Cali. "Don't look so perplexed everyone, you're giving me only ten crates of grain so what will it be. Half the supply of bamboo, syrup, or honey." As my spine continues to strain, my heartbeat pulsates in my ears. "Well?"

"Honey," Andre finally states.

"Glad we could come to an agreement, boys. Get to work." Andre and Chard promptly begin unstacking the crates onto two wheelers. Walking forward, I get ready to help. "No," Cali clamps her hand around my arm. I swallow as her hand grips tighter, like she is trying to wring the last bit of water out of a damp towel. "They do not deserve our help."

Ripping her arm away, Cali lets go of me, continuing down the dock back to the boat. Now is my chance. Muscles tense with anxiety, I search for what to say as I fixate on Chard, trying to get him to notice me with my eyes. Stepping closer, I open my mouth to speak.

"Rose!" Cali shouts over the open water. Grabbing Andre and Chard's attention, Chard and I lock eyes. "Rose!" Cali shouts again. As Andre resumes his work, Chard stays still. I keep my eyes locked with him and bring my hand to my forehead, giving Chard his classic two finger salute. A signal to show I *know* who he is. A signal I hope shows I *am* who he thinks I am. It is in this moment I see the shift in his eyes, the realization of who I am. I turn away, walking back to the boat. Confirming Chard knows it is me, I have to get him alone somehow. Joining Cali inside, my heart pounds in my ears as I wrack my brain with a plan.

"It's so hard to find good help these days," Cali exhales, rummaging through one of the coolers. I jump as she slams the lid shut, hugging alcohol in her hand. With a devilish grin she glides past me. "Come." Not wanting to piss Cali off more than she already is, I follow her to the flybridge. As she pours herself a glass, I sneak a glance to the dock as Andre and Chard move multiple crates, the thumping of the two wheelers pulsating the open air. "Don't pay them any mind," Cali scoffs. "They're not animals in a circus, they're just moving supplies back and forth." Staring at the ocean, Cali casually sips her drink.

After an hour sitting in complete silence, I realize this is how the rest of the night will go. The tension is excruciating. While Andre and Chard move supplies in and out of the boat, Cali ignores their presence. Her sense of sight and hearing have made both men blind and mute to her, neither one worth her attention. I use this to my advantage, continuously watching Chard's movements, waiting for an opportunity to present itself.

"I have to go to the bathroom," I say, placing my untouched glass down. I do not have to go, but I need to corner Chard while Cali is upstairs. Not to mention, I am absolutely freezing. My teeth chatter as the night wind grows colder. How is Cali enjoying an ice cold drink in this weather? Rushing inside, the reverberation of the two wheeler tires fill my ears.

Think, think, think.

Scouring the inside, I slither to the bathroom, keeping the door cracked slightly. I peer out, silently stalking Andre and Chard organizing new crates. There is no rain but they are pouring with sweat.

I wait as they maneuver our crates of syrup, the chiming of the glass jars filling the silent room. Before exiting, I allow them to successfully wheel the heavy crates out. Staying close behind, I watch Chard disappear into the darkness. As I step out on the deck, Chard is waiting in the shadows, quickly pulling me aside. Scanning my face, I watch as Chard's eyes bounce wildly.

"Rose?" he breathes in disbelief. "Rose Pharl?"

"Yes!" I loudly whisper. "Yes it's me!"

"What," he studies my new face. "What happened to you?"

"What happened to you?" Inches away, the concern in both our eyes glistens off the moonlight. Staring at one another, my mind surges with questions to ask him. As Andre's footsteps and rhythmic wheels fade away, I nervously swallow. "What are you doing here?" I whisper.

"It's a long story," he scoffs, a hint of sadness in his voice.

"Where are your spheres?"

"That's an even longer story," he smirks. "Why didn't you tell me you were leaving Amella?" Confusion twists my face.

"You knew I was leaving?" Chard sinks his head down, glossiness coating his blue eyes.

"Rose, I apologize," he mumbles. "I should've told you sooner."

"Told me what?" I ask, my voice distressed. The disappointment on his face is the same expression when he presented his wrist to his brother. Shamelessly showing someone stole all his points. Guilt hits me. "I'm sorry about…" I look to his sphereless face, knowing I was the one that caused this. I have been longing to apologize for what Jejune and I did to him. Now that he is here before me, I cannot do it. "What should you have told me?"

"I shouldn't have come here," Chard says, shaking his head. A lump of panic starts in my throat. What does he mean? Come where? Come here?

"Chard," I plead, taking hold of his arms. "Where are we *right* now?"

Suddenly a gust of wind blows, sending my floral crown flying. Quickly, Chard and I both reach for it, triggering the motion light above the glass sliding door. Disclosing our presence, the bulb burns like a spotlight as we stand still as statues. Both our palms firmly hold the crown as the petals continue to whip around, our bodies tightly pressed together. Both sensing it, Chard and I look up to see Cali peering over the balcony. Sipping her glass, her hair violently sways as I watch Cali glare not at us, but at me. Her blackened eyes combat the high winds, her vexed scowl persistent. Although Chard and I were only chatting, the way Cali is looking at me makes it seem like I have done something worse. Much worse. Something unforgivable.

The entire ride back my body swelled with anxiety, waiting for something to happen. The dark night. The pitch black water. The intense tension between Cali and I. When the boat finally did slow into our dock, my fearfulness of an altercation continued to build, but nothing happened. As my eyes adjust to the wall of trees and the faint outline of the truck, I silently make my way down to the dock lines.

"I'll handle it." Agreeing, I make my way to the sliding glass door. Avoiding another interrogation from the spotlight above, I keep my movements small. "You care to confess what you and that imbecile were doing?" Swallowing, I face Cali. Her pale skin looks sickly with the blue under glow glistening all around us.

"He asked if I was feeling okay." I wait for a response, but am not given one. "I told him I was sea sick earlier but I was fine." My heartbeat pounds throughout my head, muffling everything near me. I try to calm myself down. In the event she does respond, I want to be able to hear it.

"Leave the clothes you borrowed inside." Cali unlocks the latch, stepping onto the dock out of view. "And," she forcibly adds. "Don't shut the glass door. It locks automatically."

Wasting no time, I rush inside. I keep my hand on the sliding glass, contemplating if I should lock Cali out. Thinking better, I let go and snake through the narrow path of crates, carelessly removing my shawl and crown and toss them on a cooler. Not stopping, I reach my room, sealing the door firmly shut behind me. All the trust building Cali and I have done is gone.

Using the vague moonlight above, I scramble to find my backpack, propping the bag where the door meets the frame. Although it is not much, if Cali tries to enter, I will hear the scraping of my bag on the rough carpet. I should have taken a weapon with me. A knife from our kitchen. A razor from our bathroom. One of the guns, but how was I to know I would need protection to possibly defend myself. I have no idea what this woman is capable of. Her words alone cut like a sharp blade, who is to say she will not try anything. It is just her and I on this boat. My fear brings me back to that night on the wooden dock. How Jejune stabbed that night crew in the neck. Cali could do the same, letting my lifeless body fly overboard just how Jejune and I rolled the deceased night crew into the boat. For no one to see or hear.

Sinking into bed, I hug my knees, my brain wide awake as I think of Chard. Of all the places, of all the people to see. Chard? Why couldn't he tell me what happened to him? Every question I asked him was met with dismay. Except for when he apologized to me, claiming he should have told me something sooner. What did he want to confess? If anyone should have apologized it was me. He is my friend, and I lied to him. Lied about my travels, lied about his head injury, and even though I did not say anything about his stolen points, that too, is in a way a lie. But the last sentence he told me.

'*I shouldn't have come here.*'

Those five words echo in my exhausted head. Shouldn't have come where? We were hours away from Cali and I am certain not anywhere in Amella. We did not see night crew, we were traveling way past curfew, and there was no one except for Andre and Chard. Who both had no dark makeup or spheres under their eyes. We traded at a totally secluded and unpopulated location. Some sort of island Andre mentioned. Where *were* we?

Completely overwhelmed, I bury my face in between my knees, hugging them tighter. Holding back tears, I pick my head up, looking to the stars. Reminding myself that I am not alone. I am looking at the same sky as my dad tonight. I should have stayed with Chard, I could have found a way to get back to the North. I missed the perfect opportunity to go home. Regretful, I push down my emotions as my eyes lock back onto the door.

Before long, the stars above fade like chalk being washed by rain, replaced with the early morning hue. My body relaxes as I realize I am okay. If Cali were to do something she would have already done it. With the motion of a sloth, I wander across the room, removing my make shift security system. Dragging my backpack, I yawn and swing my door open.

"Good morning!" I tense my grip around the doorknob as I stare at Cali, her aged face grinning wildly. "You don't look like you slept well. Let's get started, shall we?" I watch Cali leave, acting like last night did not occur.

Filled with anxiety, exhaustion, and now confusion, I head to the bathroom. I slap cold water on my face, hoping the sudden temperature change will wake me up. Dragging my hands over my eyes, I feel the uneven surface on either side of my face. Three bumps under my left eye, none under my right eye. Like brushing paint on a canvas, I graze the same spot over and over, feeling only smooth skin. A hint of sadness strikes me. Those three other spheres have been with me my entire life; I kind of miss them. Finally looking at my reflection, I am perplexed to see my dark makeup has faded to a lighter shade of black. Not bothering to change my clothes, I join Cali outside, the bright sunlight quickly drying out my chilled face.

"I think my makeup is fading," I say, approaching Cali.

"It's from the salt water. The makeup reacts to the sodium chloride in our tears," she explains. "It's a slow process, but with the salt in the air, our makeup is fading much quicker." Examining Cali's eyes, I realize her makeup is also lighter. "We can put more on at tomorrow's ceremony." I simply nod; so the makeup is not permanent.

Cali and I perform the same routine. Grab crate. Carry crate. Climb ramp. Unload. Grab crate. Carry crate. Climb ramp. Unload. It does not take long for me to regret pulling an all nighter. I let my mind get the best of me, and my body is paying for it. Thankfully, there are less crates we received than Cali gave, making the loading process easier on my arms and knees.

Sweat outlines my face as we bring the last crates into the truck. Although just fabric, my shoulders strain as I slowly follow Cali, her also struggling with the crates. I guess thin cloth piled on top of one another eventually adds up. Finished, Cali closes the roll up door as I enjoy the occan breeze.

"That was fast," she exhales. "Is your bag packed?"

"Yes," I reply, still waiting for Cali's kindness to be replaced with her anger from last night.

"Excellent." She makes her way onto the dock. "I'll grab your bag."

"No, I can –"

"Could you start the truck while I head to the engine room and lock up?"

Frozen, I stare at Cali handing me a set of keys. The same set Forest used to lock the trailer door. The same set Cali used to open the glass door. Now, the same set used to start the truck. I must have been too nervous when I was driving the truck to notice the keys were right in front of me.

"Sure," I respond, gingerly reaching out for them.

"It's the one with the T initial."

Racing to the truck, I examine the keys, studying the brass and bronze metal. My excited feet fling sand as my fingers flip through each one. Hoisting myself up,

I plop down in the driver seat, spreading the keys like a deck of cards. I read the engravement of each one.

T, Y, T, D, B.

One T must be for the truck. The other T must be for the trailer. My eyes shift between Y and B. Y for yacht or B for boat. What did Cali refer to it as? I stare at the fifth key, the concaved D shining brightly. I search my brain for what the D could go to. Hearing the swoosh of the glass door, I fumble with the keys. Trying the first metallic gold T, I jam the key into the ignition but it does not fit. I flip to the other T and it smoothly slides into the ignition as I quickly blast the air conditioning.

First T for trailer, second T for truck.

Hopping out of the driver's seat, I meet Cali at the back of the truck. I take my bag from her as she walks past me.

"Thanks again," I spit out, getting Cali to turn around. "For bringing me along." I face the sea, thinking of the best way to phrase my question. "Sorry for getting sick on the…" I point to the ship. "Boat or yacht?" I keep my head forward, hoping Cali's answer is the clue I need.

"Yacht," Cali states. "A boat over thirty five feet is considered a yacht." I lower my finger and nod, receiving the confirmation I needed.

First T for trailer, second T for truck. Y for yacht.

Mesmerized, I walk to the passenger side, gawking at the ocean. Being in the North's bubble all my life, I was naïve to the rest of the world. A world full of beauty. Similar to the first morning I saw the water, it is calm, the small curls of low tide splashing against the shore. Driving away, I look through Cali's window at the water one last time, but I know this will not be the last time. I will come to the ocean again, with my mom, just like she hoped for.

Disoriented, I open my eyes. My vision adjusts to the darkness as I remember I am in the truck. I must have been out for a long time. Uncurling my spine, I sit up straight, my neck stiff from hanging over my seatbelt.

"Sleep well?" Cali asks.

"Yeah. Guess I slept through my turn. Want me to drive?"

"No that's alright." Cali smiles, quickly looking at me, then to the road. "We're almost back anyway." Almost back, was I out for that long? Ears filling with the tires running over gravel, I look at the CD collection in the center console, debating which artist to play. "Why did you lie?"

"Lie?" I question.

"About your occupation. About being an actress."

"I did not lie," I defend. "You assumed." I stare at Cali, trying to make out her facial expression from the backlight of the headlights.

"Then enlighten me. Why is a boom operator wearing actress makeup?" My mind races to concoct an explanation. "And why did you shave and dye your hair?"

"I wanted to." Standing my ground, I keep my focus on Cali.

"You wouldn't happen to shave it so a wig could fit over it?" My throat dries as I try to speak. How would she know that?

"How would you know that?" I mutter out loud. Swallowing, I take a risk with my next statement. "Wila mentioned you are from Amella. Did you grow up there? Were you an actress?" My heartbeat floods my eardrums as I continue to pry. "She said you had to leave."

123

"Wila does not know what she's talking about," Cali snaps, tensing her grip on the steering wheel. "I'm sure she told you about her memory, it's not so great." She quickly laughs, her smile appearing and vanishing in the same second. "Don't take anything that woman says seriously."

"But she is your –"

"She's an acquaintance," Cali spits. "That is all." As the truck speeds along, I look out the windshield to the dark road; I should have played that CD when I had the chance. The truck rides over a bump as Cali and I bounce slightly. The movement sends the crates in the back shifting and the keys in the ignition rattling. My eyes switch from Cali's face to the keys.

"I know about your keys." My words hang in the air as Cali says nothing. "I know each one goes to something." Snapping my head back to Cali, her neck strains, veins popping out like tree roots sprouting on the surface. Seeing as she will not respond, I change the subject to another topic that has weighed on my mind. "Did you ever see Pete that day," taking it upon myself to ask the questions.

"Pete? Pete who?" Cali vigorously shakes her head.

"The woodworker about the oak slabs."

"Yes, that's why we only took four," Cali scoffs. "The fifth one wasn't going to be sanded in time." As the veins in her neck recede, I stare at her as irritation infuses my shoulders. Now she is the one lying.

"I know about the bullet." I firmly state. "I know about a lot." My voice rises, hoping my louder tone will make Cali understand. "I know the bullet was recent. I know bartering doesn't get you a sixteen foot truck and a yacht." Adrenaline pumps through my blood as I continue to spit facts her way. "And Cali. Is that your real name or is it from the sign –"

Ceasing my rambling, Cali slams on the brakes hard. We both shift forward as I fumble to grab the dashboard. Cali springs back up, slamming both her palms against the wheel. Gaining momentum, Cali flings her hands up and pounds on the wheel three more times, her draped arms violently shaking. Frightened, I press my back against the cold door behind me.

"I don't appreciate the sudden interrogation!" Cali screams. She rests her palms on the wheel, slowly wrapping each finger one by one over the gray leather. "I took you in, I fed you, I gave you a place to stay, I made you feel welcome!" She removes her hand from the wheel, brushing her long hair out of her face. "I don't like being lied to!" I remain frozen, eyeing Cali's breathing as her dark eyes glare my way, like a wolf stalking its prey. "I heard what you and that idiot were talking about on the yacht." My bones stiffen as her eyes widen, unblinking as I helplessly stare. "You asked him where you were." My shoulders fall slightly with relief. She did not hear Chard and I's whole conversation. She frowns and shakes her head. "Big mistake Rose." Exhaling loudly, Cali lifts her foot off the brake, beginning to drive again.

"I was curious," I sincerely state.

"I told you to let me do the talking," Cali hisses. "Curiosity gets you killed. Be thankful I have connections." Processing Cali's words, I continue, hoping she can answer the question Chard did not have a chance to.

"So where were we?" I ask.

"We were at the trade run."

"But where?" I pry, body still tense.

"Off the coast."

"Where specifically?" Why is she being so vague?

The truck slows as I see the warm glow of Cali's tents. Coming to a stop, Cali turns off the ignition as we sit outside the wall of trailers in silence. Unbuckling, she shifts to face her entire body towards me, looking at me head on. Remaining stoic, I stay pressed up against the door as my nerves swell. "Tomorrow we'll unload and then you're done."

"Done?" I peep.

"Off the project, it isn't a good fit. You're too much of a liability." Cali provides a sympathetic smile. "I hope you understand." I do not respond, realizing any attempt to defend myself is not worth my time or energy. If she wants me off the special project, so be it. I will soon be leaving for Amella. I reach for my bag as Cali opens her door, heading to her luxurious porch. Parting ways, I keep my head down as my shoes stomp hard on the dry ground, missing how they would sink into the fine sand at the ocean. "I should have known," Cali loudly sighs, drawing my attention to her across the way. Head hung back, her long hair resembles a waterfall as she presents her face to the moon above. "It's in your name." A small chuckle erupts from her mouth, her laughter echoing in the dark. "Rose," she breathes into the night air. "All roses have thorns."

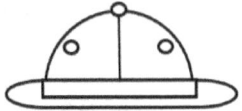

Matching the darkness outside, I brush open our tent curtain to the lights off. I tip toe, the soft breathing of Jejune and Stevey down the hall reaching my ears. Not wanting to wake them, I sneak towards the couch. As I sink into the cushions, my mind becomes hazy, exhaustion taking hold. Not putting up a battle, I let my tired mind and body rest, joining in the darkness of the room and night.

***

"Rose." I feel the light tapping of fingers on my arm. Turning over, I open my eyes to see Stevey. He takes his hand off my arm as a big smile fills his small face. "How was your trip?" Looking down, I see someone placed a blanket over my body, remembering I knocked out on the couch; I even left my dirty shoes on.

"It was good," I smile towards Stevey. The memory of Cali loudly pounding on the steering wheel erases my smile. The pure aggression she had in her outburst all because I asked a few questions she did not want to answer. There is no need for a grown woman to throw a toddler temper tantrum. Feeling Stevey's fingers tap on me again, I look to him sitting criss cross, scrunching his green eyes under his crooked glasses. "What Stevey?"

"Did you get to see more mountains?" Sitting up, I swing my legs off the couch as Stevey hops up next to me.

"I did not see mountains," I reply. As I say the words, I am reminded of what I did see. I did see Chard. I saw him and did not seize an opportunity. Pushing that aside, I continue to share with Stevey. "But I did see the ocean." His jaw lets gravity take hold as he opens his mouth in shock.

"The ocean!" he squeals. I nod and swallow a yawn as his eyes grow wide. "What does *that* look like?"

"It is like a river, but much bigger. It has waves that crash on the shore and it is the prettiest blue." As I continue my description, my mom comes to mind. "It is best in the morning, when the sun shines on the water."

"I have to add that!" Stevey shouts, running down the hallway. Yawning, I quickly rub my eyes as Stevey's footsteps echo back into the main room. "This is the only blue I have." Focusing on Stevey, I watch him hunch over the table, scribbling on a piece of paper. Peeking over his shoulder, I realize he is coloring on his map. The same map that we used to venture here. The same map that started this whole journey. "Like that?"

Tossing the paper in my face, I study Stevey's updated map. Bones tightening, my eyes look to a long strip of land added to the edge of the West on his map labeled CALI written in capital letters. Adjacent to that are swirls of blue representing the ocean I described.

"Just like that," I finally respond. I stare at the map, entranced with the new landmarks as my mind flashes to the map at North Amella. "Where is Jejune?" I ask, changing the subject.

"She's at work," Stevey says, placing his map back on the table.

"Shouldn't you be in school?"

"Yeah, but you looked cold. You didn't have a blanket so I grabbed mine for you to use." I look to the blanket, realizing that it is his.

"Thank you Stevey," I grin.

"I'm gonna go to school now." Stevey lunges into me, wrapping his arms around me. "I missed you."

Before I can hug him back, he jumps off the couch and rushes out the tent.

I watch as his wild blonde hair bounces with each step. My eyes flick down, focusing once again on Stevey's map. The four dark letters spelling CALI hypnotize me, reminding me where I am. I shift my gaze to the other States, finding the North. My bones relax looking at the Northern territory, realizing I am not trapped in CALI. I am merely a few states away. Exhaling, I lay back down. Unsure when Cali wants to unload the truck, I tug Stevey's blanket to my chin, closing my eyes once again.

***

After my short morning nap, I cautiously make my way outside the trailers. I am beyond nervous about how today is going to go. As much as I want to keep asking questions, I know not to. Putting my hat over my head, I sneak a glance to Cali pulling out the loading ramp. I am hoping for bubbly theatrical Cali, but after her comment about roses having thorns last night, I think she may still have that mentality today.

"We'll start with the coolers," she says, not making eye contact with me. Although I am not greeted with her usual good morning, she is not punching my skull in like she did to the steering wheel last night. I will take the cold shoulder and no eye contact for our last day working together over that.

Following her into the truck, we begin with the dozens of coolers. Rather than store the coolers in a trailer, we carry each one to the kitchen tent. Cali informs me not to open the coolers as they are sealed air tight with dry ice to keep the meat fresh. She really was not lying when she said meat was shipped here. Next we unload the grains, which are not in the best packaging. As the sun sizzles, I carefully balance the opened burlaps of ingredients. Flour, wheat, rice, various seeds and nuts. I hold one bag in each hand, palms wetting with sweat.

Hiking up the loading ramp, my footsteps echo in the almost empty truck. Waiting for Cali's instructions, I heave over the fabric crates; I should have brought water with me today. Grossly, I remove my damp hat, allowing the small hairs on my head to breathe. Good thing I did not wear my floral crown today, my sweat would have ruined it. As my neck hangs down, a droplet of sweat drips from my head off my chin, seeping into the cloth fabric below me. Panicked, I quickly wipe the moisture away as my hand brushes over the hard material. Expecting my palm to sink into soft fabric, I am perplexed when it hits something firm. Like flipping a page in a book, I lift the bottom corner of the fabric to see a white plastic bag. As I peel back the fabric more, Cali's footsteps climbing the loading ramp stop me. I instantly let go and step away, waiting in the middle of the truck. My moist palms nervously clench my damp hat as I stand in the hot vehicle.

"Let's get late breakfast, shall we?" she smiles.

"What about these?" I ask, gesturing to the fabric lining the perimeter.

"Just leave those," she disregards. "They aren't perishable so they won't spoil in the heat." Cali turns her back to me, making her way down the loading ramp. In one swift motion, I flick my wrist, tossing my hat next to the crate. Avoiding eye contact, I join Cali as she reaches above her, closing the roll up door. As my feet pound down the loading ramp, my heartbeat pounds in my head. There is something going on here. The bullet. The keys. The secretive trade run. Now a mysterious plastic bag in a crate of fabric. I cannot just accuse on a hunch, I do not need another repeat of last night's interrogation. I have to look through that crate and confirm what I saw. Now I have an excuse, I simply left my hat in the truck. Tomorrow morning, I will get my hat. Tomorrow morning, I will get back in that truck.

I did not attend the ceremony last night. I slept and I needed the sleep. Although I did not get a reapplication of makeup, I do not want any. Drying off after my shower this morning, I wiped under my eyes to see my white towel stained with a dark smear. I may still have black makeup under my eyes, but it is not as bold, as if my relationship with Cali is dwindling.

With all the rest I got, I was able to wake up right at the start of communal breakfast. Exiting the tent, I glance towards the packed breakfast area. As the majority of everyone, and more importantly, Cali are distracted, I sneak out of the living quarters and past the trailers. To my surprise, the roll up door to the truck is already open. Hesitant, I look around, but see no sight of anyone. With the loading ramp closed, I kick my leg up and climb inside. Creeping over to the crates, I see my hat is right where I threw it yesterday. Bending down, I grab my hat and spring back up. Nervous, I look out of the truck to see no one, only sand stretching on to meet the red stained mountains.

Just like yesterday, I lift the corner to see a white plastic bag. I drag the rest of the fabric, unveiling a layer of multiple white plastic bags. Curious, I raise the fabric of another crate to see the same thing; no wonder these crates were extremely heavy. Leaning in, I see the bags are filled with round smooth pebbles. Heart racing, I sneak another glance out of the truck to see the same view of sand and mountains. Pushing my luck, I pick one of the bags up to get a closer look. The bag is dense and packed full of pebbles. Dissecting the bag, I realize the bag itself is not white, but the contents within are white and the packaging is clear. Crammed together, I make out these are not white pebbles, but white pills.

"What are you doing here?"

Frozen with fear, I do not move. Anxiety punches every nerve in my body as my feet stay glued to the floor, my hands hovering in front of me holding the bag. Muscles mummified, my eyes move to look out of the back of the truck, only to see the sand and mountains.

"Nice to see you too," a man states.

Quiet as humanly possible, I place the bag down, fold the fabric over, and tip toe to the back of the truck. I can confirm Cali is outside, but I do not know the voice of the man. Debating whether I should jump or not, my foot dangles off the truck. Thankfully I retract my foot back and cling to the edge of the truck. If I were to jump, the sound of my feet colliding with the ground would be too loud. Staying put, I listen.

"You were missed at the run," Cali says. "You shouldn't be here Timothy."

Timothy? Timothy from the trade run?

"I know, but I left to come here," he reassures.

"Here?" Cali questions. I press my cheek against the truck, popping my ear out to hear their conversation. I cannot tell where they are, but it sounds like the front of the truck.

"There was an alert the alarm went off, are they here?"

"Are who here?" Cali kindly asks.

"Three fugitives, from the North. Two girls and a young boy."

"Fugitives?"

"Yes, for evading Counting Day." Panic punches my body. It was only a matter of time before there would be consequences for our absence. "And possible murder." My heart nearly stops as Timothy's words elongate over the desert air.

"We haven't had any newcomers in a while," Cali innocently replies.

"Did anyone cross?"

"No. We would have followed protocol if –"

"But the alarm –"

"Children," Cali abruptly shouts. "A few children strayed too far. Besides, that was weeks ago." A long silence fills the air as I anxiously listen.

"You know the repercussions for hiding fugitives," he states.

"Of course, but we're not."

"But Veil –"

"If Veil is so concerned then Veil can come to Cali to see with their own eyes." My mind immediately recognizes the name. That is the same name that drunk blonde said on Counting Day. That is the same name that Aster said when doing my makeup.

Who is Veil?

"Cali, this is very serious. You know what they'll do –"

"Are you questioning my authority, Timothy?" Cali asks.

"No, but Cali, you know what they'll do. I came here to warn you –"

"It sounds like you are," Cali states. "If so, these products can stay here."

Products?

"No. Apologies Cali. We would never question your authority."

"That's splendid to hear. I would hate to end our agreement."

Agreement?

"As would we Cali."

"I do hope you mean that. Would you like to confirm? The products are already loaded."

Crap!

"Yes. Let me start up the truck so it is nice and cool for the ride back."

Softly, I leap to the other side of the truck, waiting for my opportunity. As the vehicle rumbles to a start, I jump, the engine masking my hard landing. Pressing my back tight against the truck's exterior like I am scaling the side of a building, I quietly creep away. I seal my mouth closed, breathing out of my nose as Cali, Timothy, and I play a game of cat and mouse. Reaching the front passenger tire, I crouch down to confirm when they are inside the truck.

I search under the truck for their presence. My eyes pinpoint Cali's long garments covering her shoes as she unlatches the loading ramp. Then my eyes shift to Timothy. Disbelief piles onto me, physically pushing on my body, sinking my knees and palms lower into the ground. Locked in place, I do not break my sight with Timothy's footwear as the miniscule grains of desert sand embed into my skin. The matte black color rises up his legs to meet thick black pants. Resenting the doubt filling my mind, I truly want to not believe my own eyes, but I know I am not mistaken. I would recognize those boots anywhere. Those are not just random black boots. Those are the same boots that shined bright off the Counting Day stage. Those are the same boots that shined bright off my flashlight on the wooden dock. Those are Amella crew member boots. As Timothy's crew member boots slam against the loading ramp, my mind screams at me to run.

I push off the ground and round the front of the truck. I race through the trailers, slowing down to a jog when I reach the breakfast area. Frantic, I scan the tables until my eyes find Jejune. Once they do, I speed walk to her, my breath heavy as I reach her side.

"Good morning sunshine," Jejune jokes, looking up from her seat.

"Can I talk to you," I state, almost out of breath.

"Sure, let me finish my –"

"Now," I plead. I glance to the fishermen, then back to Jejune, quickly raising my eyebrows. She puts her food down as I wring the hat in my hands.

"Gentlemen," Jejune smirks, swinging her legs over the picnic bench. "I shall return in –" I yank Jejune's arm, pulling her away before she can finish. Booking it to the living quarters, I drag her along. "Rose, what the –"

"Just get to the tent," I instruct, hustling down the path.

"What's going on!" she yells, flinching her arm out of my grip.

"Lower your voice!" I softly shout. "Cali knows."

"Knows what?" Jejune exclaims, following me into our tent.

"She knows about the night crew," I whisper, closing the entrance to our tent as soon as she is inside.

"Night crew?" Jejune furrows, scrunching the skin above her nose.

"Cali knows we killed crew members," I pant. "We are fugitives."

"What are you talking about Rose?"

"They know who we are and they are coming for us." I blurt out. "Amella is here right now." Jejune stares at me, not responding. "And, I know this is going to sound crazy, but I saw Chard." Jejune's emerald eyes slant with confusion.

"Chard?"

"Yes, he was at the trade run. We were on some kind of secret island." As Jejune's eyebrows relax back to normal, a smirk forms on her lips.

"I think that sunburn is messing with your head," Jejune laughs.

"Listen to me!" Frustrated, I close my eyes. I know she is one for jokes, but now is not the time. Exhaling, I open my eyes. "What are we going to do?"

"What are we going to do about what?"

"About *this*," I stress, widening my eyes.

"There's nothing to worry about," she shrugs.

"We are fugitives Jejune." What is she not understanding?

"If we were fugitives, we'd be in trouble," Jejune scoffs. "And we aren't in trouble."

"Rose and Jejune," Cali sternly states outside the tent. On cue, Jejune and I both snap our heads to the closed tent entrance. "Meet me in my tent. I need to speak with both of you now."

Jejune and I do not move, waiting until Cali's footsteps completely fade away. Snapping her neck, Jejune looks to me.

"Now do you believe me," I spit, a hint of aggravation in my voice. I toss my hat onto the counter, waiting for Jejune to speak. Not responding, Jejune flings the curtain open and exits the tent. "Where are you going?"

"Cali wants to see us," she calmly replies. "So let's go."

"We need a plan," I whisper, staying close to Jejune.

"Let's just go with it."

"Go with it?" I stare at Jejune. "I do not think that is the best idea."

"Winging it has gotten us this far." She smirks, hitching her eyebrows up. "Hasn't failed us yet."

Jejune stops and I face forward, realizing we have made it to Cali's tent. I search my brain for something to say but Jejune's hand has already connected with the fabric. Walking inside, Cali gestures for us to sit. Silently, we take our seats like two students in trouble sentenced to the school principal's office. I glance towards Jejune as she crosses her arms, sinking into the elegant antique chair. Turning my attention to Cali, I watch as she paces behind the desk. Although there is a soft smile on her face, I can tell she is angry. Done pacing, Cali exhales, placing her boney fingers on the wood.

"Did you kill crew members?" Cali calmy asks.

"That's a big accusation," Jejune states.

"A big accusation but a warranted one." She flutters her eyes closed. "I'm going to ask you again," opening her eyes. "Did you kill crew members." Not wanting a repeat of the steering wheel incident, I stare at Cali's palms pressed on top of the desk, as if I am attempting to keep them there.

"I mean," Jejune exhales. Breaking my trance with Cali's hands, I turn towards Jejune as she looks to the ceiling. "When you say –"

"Did you!" Cali screams, slamming her hands on the table. I lean back slightly, the sound of her outburst pushing my body. Eyes closed, she stands up straight, plastering a smile on her face. Cali snaps her eyelids open. "Well." Seeing as Cali already knows the truth, I respond.

"Yes. In self defense."

"Are we in danger?" Jejune questions. Uncrossing her arms, Jejune sits up, the seriousness of the situation hitting her.

"No," Cali shakes her head, face softening. "No, you're safe here."

"How can you be so sure," I ask.

"I'm sure," she snaps at me, losing the softness in her face. "While you're both here," she says, gesturing to us. "Is there anything else you need to confess to." Like a pendulum, Cali's eyes bounce back and forth between Jejune and I. I look to Jejune, her head sunken.

"Nothing more we need to confess," I reply.

"It's now or never," she emphasizes, her eyes growing wide.

"Nothing more," I repeat, looking directly at her.

"Thank you for your honesty." Tension in the air, she begins to show herself out. "All is forgiven."

"Are you sure we aren't in danger," Jejune asks again.

"They need us," Cali firmly states. "They would never do anything to break our trust," she walks towards the entrance of her tent. "Never," she repeats, brushing the tent curtain and exiting. I hold my mouth open, waiting for the curtain to completely close before speaking.

"Jejune she knows," I stress.

"And she said all is forgiven," Jejune shrugs.

"You believe her?"

"Yes, why wouldn't I?" Bewildered, I stare at Jejune, trying to understand what is going on with her.

"What's going on with you?" I exclaim, straining my face.

"What do you mean?"

"Why aren't you more skeptical. Why aren't you being… you!" I shout, shakily thrusting my hands out towards her for emphasis.

"I am me," she laughs.

"No, no you are not," I cry. "You are a totally different Jejune."

"Why because I'm enjoying myself here," she rebuttals with attitude.

"Enjoying?" I nervously laugh. "We are not safe here. She said they need us. *They* being Amella. Cali and Amella are not separate." I take a breath as my face warms with frustration. "They are obviously working together or something. Amella came here for supplies, and now we are fugitives." As I ramble on, Jejune places her elbow on the arm of her chair, rubbing her eyes. "You're going to take her word for it," I state, watching Jejune continue to ignore me. "How do we know –"

"You done?" Jejune shouts, springing her head up. I look to Jejune, her jaw clenched and eyes wide.

"Don't be blinded because Stevey is happy." I seal my lips together tight as I hear the words escape my mouth. Disappointed with myself, I slowly blink as I see Jejune's face sink.

"Don't weaponize Stevey against me," she hisses through her teeth.

"I'm not," I weakly exhale. "I would never, it's just…" I shake my head, instantly regretting what I said. No amount of apologizing will take back those words. Just how her scar used to pierce through me when she was angry, my words just did the same, cutting deep through her. The difference being, when Jejune's scar cut through me, I would see the knife coming. The words I just uttered were unwarranted; my knife was unexpected.

"You coming to Stevey's birthday party?" Shocked, I lift my head back up, looking to Jejune.

"Of course."

"Then we'll see each other then."

Glued to her, my eyes follow as she leaves. Encompassed alone in Cali's tent, I remain in the chair, defeatedly gazing at the chaos around me. Staring at the clutter, I am taken back to Fred and Frank's cabin when Jejune stormed off, questioning if I ever cried, leaving me isolated with a swirl of emotions. Just like that day, Jejune has stormed off again, my only company dim lighting, stacked boxes, and walls camouflaged with sphereless faces of the past. Weird how history repeats itself.

Spending the majority of my life with top sphere holders, not one person I interacted with seemed depressed. Even if they were, they had a good way of hiding their true feelings. For the first time, I am feeling that way, and I do not think I am hiding it well. Between the status of Jejune and I's relationship, Cali no longer trusting me, not apologizing to Chard, missing my parents deeply, it has finally taken a toll. The solution to this feeling is not a nine year old's birthday party, but it will be a nice distraction.

Preoccupied by my own sorrow, I forgot to get Stevey a present. Scrambling last minute, I came up with an idea I hope he likes. But like all children his age, they say the first opinion that pops in their mind. Kids can be brutally honest without realizing it. As my ears fill with laughter and light conversation, I arrive to Stevey's birthday party. The last celebration I attended was Counting Day. Walking into the ballroom, smiling with Chard, having light conversation just like the others around me are doing now. Then it changed drastically. Gunshots, screaming, fear. Joy traded for dread. It seems like a distant memory. Quickly snapping out of it, I grin as Stevey and a bunch of his classmates come rushing towards me.

"Happy birthday Stevey," I say, my grin growing into a smile.

"Thanks! I'm nine now!" he beams. "I made her that crown," he says to the classmates surrounding him. I briefly chuckle, touching the floral petals resting on my head. Of course I had to wear my crown for his special day.

"I got you a present." Stevey and his posse of classmates stare with anticipation as he takes the small bag. He whips his head around, searching the breakfast area that has been transformed for his celebration.

"JJ!" he squeals. "Can I open this one now?"

"Sure baby," she smiles, walking towards us. We both remain quiet as he hastily reaches inside the gift bag, finally revealing his present. Stevey and his classmates gawk at the beautiful opal shell in his hand.

"A sea shell from the ocean," I say. Back at the trade run, I collected a handful for my mom. I am sure she would not mind if I gave one to her favorite student.

"That's so cool!" one of the boys next to Stevey shouts.

"Can I hold it?" another classmate shouts. Not answering, Stevey runs towards me, giving me a big hug.

"I'm gonna keep it forever," his voice muffled as his face squishes into my jacket. Releasing from our embrace, he looks up and we lock eyes. "We can find more tomorrow!"

"Tomorrow?" I question.

"When we go camping." Confused, I stare into his green eyes through his glasses. "JJ," he pouts, making his way to her. "You said you would ask."

"I forgot baby, I'm sorry," she responds, delicately brushing his neatly parted and slicked back hair.

"Can we see it," the classmate begs again. Stevey joins his classmates and they scurry off, each passing the shell around. Overlooking the decorations, Jejune and I stay silent. No banter. No small talk. Nothing, like we are strangers to one another. My heart pounds with uncomfortableness.

"Stevey wanted to go on a camping trip for his birthday," Jejune says, breaking the silence. "Climb the mountains, go fishing, a little getaway. You, me, and him." Surprised, I look to Jejune. Stevey wants me to go on this trip too? At the current state of Jejune and I's friendship? I guess Stevey does not see it, or chooses not to see it. Innocence or ignorance. "I understand if you don't wanna go." She keeps her gaze forward, her hat shielding the profile of her face. "You kept your promise of staying until his birthday and I'm more than grateful for that." Jejune looks down. "I know going back will make you happy so you should." Although going back will make me happy, I continue to stare at Jejune. Her sunken head hangs like a weeping willow.

"I'll think about it," I reply. Jejune tilts her head up. The setting sun reflects the glossiness coating Jejune's eyes.

"Please do. It'll be nice to have one last adventure." Jejune weakly smiles as I struggle to do the same. Jejune always puts on a brave face, even when she does not feel brave. We do not need to exchange words to know we are both suppressing the sad truth she has just confirmed. If I leave, she will not be joining me.

Thunderous claps erupt as the entire population of Cali gathers around Stevey. Grinning ear to ear, he gyrates with excitement as River and a few other cacao workers balance the main dessert. As requested, Stevey got his chocolate cake. Joining, Jejune and I make our way to the breakfast area. Disguising myself in the crowd, I hang back as Jejune stands next to Stevey.

Carefully, River places the rich cake in front of Stevey, the candles glowing off of his glasses and cheerful face. On cue, everyone sings happy birthday. As we sing, Stevey raises his shoulders to his ears, his eyes bouncing back and forth like a finger rapidly flicking on and off a light switch. Smiling, I continue singing with the chorus of Cali filling the air.

"… happy birthday to you!" we all conclude. A frown melts away Stevey's smile. Panicked, Jejune slides into the picnic table beside him.

"What's wrong baby?" she asks. Stevey swipes his arms around Jejune and collides into her.

"Thank you JJ," he cries, not letting her go. Relief allows Jejune's body to sink down, hugging him back, holding him so tight. There was nothing wrong; Stevey was simply overwhelmed with joy. As Jejune and Stevey squeeze one another, their love can be felt by everyone around.

"Blow out your candles and make a wish little man," Jejune instructs, finally releasing from their embrace. Straightening out his glasses, his gleefulness returns as he leans back, winding up for the big moment. Stevey swivels his head, extinguishing all the small flames. Cheers and applause echo as streams of smoke wiggle up off the candles.

Frozen in time, I catch myself staring at Stevey, his joyfulness taking hold over me. How could I possibly be expected to say no to his birthday camping trip. Contemplating the decision I have to make, I let others pass as they await their slice of cake. Jejune is right, it would be nice to have one last adventure. This whole journey has been an adventure, but it would be nice to finish how it all started. Just the three of us. I can stay for one last time because it may truly be the last time. Seeing how proud Jejune was to give Stevey his best birthday ever is more than enough confirmation that if I go back, it will only be me who does. I hope my parents can understand why I had to stay a little longer. For the chance to have a repeat of the good old times. Exploring nature, catching fish, sharing laughs. Might be false hope, but to me, it is worth a try.

Stevey was beyond thrilled to find me packing a bag for the camping trip. Rounding up clothes, Stevey rambles on how each day will go. Day one will be climbing the mountain. Day two will be sea shell hunting. Day three will be our journey back. Now that I am no longer working on the special project, I have all the time I want. It will be a change of scenery and mindfulness being away from Cali. Cali the place and Cali the person.

As we begin our day one journey, Jejune informs me that we are just walking to the lookout Cali took us to on our tour. No hiking. No strenuous trails. In Stevey's eye though, we will be 'climbing the mountain'. Upon arriving to the lookout area, Jejune and I set up the tent as Stevey gleams with joy. Although I am not too keen on sleeping on the ground, it is a relief to have a tent overhead with a fluffy sleeping bag. Much better than the times we slept in the woods to get here.

Waking up on day two of our trip, I quietly sneak out of the tent as Jejune and Stevey snuggle in their sleep. The soft perennial petals tickle my palms as I brush over the delicate flowers and enjoy the sunrise. Shades of coral and gold hover over the mountain tops as the sun tries to break through the clouds. I used to think the skyscrapers of North Amella held the most beauty. Shimmering chandeliers. Exquisite marble. Still breathtaking, but those are manmade beauties. They do not compare to the feeling I get when I overlook these mountains; it is a new found beauty. Nature can be so simple yet have such a profound effect.

Once Jejune and Stevey awaken, we deconstruct the tent and head down the mountain towards the river. Jejune quizzes Stevey on his spelling as the sun slowly slides to the center of the sky. Wedged between mountains, the towering rocks shield us in from both sides as Jejune steers the boat down the narrow river. Humming across the water, we slow at an inlet, the motor dwindling to a stop. The teal water is shallow as it meets the rocky ground, stretching on to shape a short cave.

"This is so cool!" Stevey giggles, his eyes wide staring at the landscape. "Do you think there are sea shells?" he questions, turning his head to Jejune and I.

"You'll have to explore and find out," Jejune smirks. Rustling the boat, Stevey hops out and runs to the shoreline, his excited feet flinging water into the air. Wasting no time, Stevey crouches down over the colorful rocks, eagerly searching for shells. "You know," Jejune states. "Stevey wanted to celebrate on the river because that was his favorite time getting here." Favorite time? Our time on the river was arguably my worst time of the entire journey. Funny how two people can experience the same situation completely different. "I may be wrong, but," Jejune tilts her head towards me, eyebrows raised. "I don't think it was our favorite time."

"Definitely not," I shake my head, a laugh escaping both our mouths.

"JJ!" Stevey skips to the boat, hands full of rocks. "Can I play my music?" Nodding, Jejune leans over, reaching for her bag. "I haven't found any shells yet," he says to me, dumping the rocks he compiled into the boat.

"I think you will," I respond, Stevey and I sharing a smile.

"Here you go," Jejune announces, finally retrieving what Stevey was asking for. Stevey reaches for it but Jejune pulls her arm back. "Woah!" she chuckles, furrowing her brows. "What do you say?"

"Thank you, may I *please* have it?" he begs.

"Yes you may," Jejune smiles, handing over the device. "And just," she emphasizes, recoiling her arm back, "because you're a year older, does not mean you lose your manners. Okay?"

"Okay," he responds. "Can I *please* have it now?" he whines.

"Where did you get that Stevey?" I ask intrigued.

"Fred gave it to me." He presses a button and sounds of instruments flow from the device. "It's a music player. Fred made it and told me all about it."

"He told you?" I question, sneaking a glance to Jejune. During our time at Fred and Frank's cabin, Fred was not much of a talker.

"Yeah!" Stevey puts the device in his pocket. "We talked a lot."

"You and Fred *talked*?" Jejune asks mirroring my confused expression.

"We did," he smiles. "He said I didn't make him nervous. He said most people make him nervous. He said I was his friend so he gave me it." Ending the conversation, the melody fades away as Stevey runs to the shore.

As Stevey's music softly plays over the area, Jejune and I eat lunch. Chewing my meal, Jejune contently watches Stevey collect more rocks. My mind flashes to the last time Jejune and I were in a boat on a river. It was serene just like it is now. Jejune's hat is once again backwards, the sunlight acting like a spotlight under her eyes. Only this time, there is no ruby scar to enlighten, only deep black makeup. The only remnant of her scar is the bloodshot corner of her eye. I turn away from her face, guilt washing over me. I remember how badly I wanted to solve that mystery, to discover the origin of her scar. How much tension I built in my mind. Once again, I fill my mind with that same tension, still tempted to ask her about her scar.

"I'm no dumbass," Jejune says. Catching me off guard, I look to her, pushing my thoughts aside. "I know I haven't been the best to you." She grinds down her sandwich, still staring straight ahead. "Guess I got wrapped up in the Cali clan."

"It's okay," I say, placing my food down.

"It's not," Jejune spits, putting her hand up. Trying to relax, she brings her hand down, taking a deep breath. "As much as I love Stevey, it's always been me and him. I wouldn't trade *anything* for Stevey, but," she stops, her eyes flicking down. "You never raised anyone, you don't have to care for anyone. Raising Stevey by myself, it gets lonely. Being with others who raise kids on their own here, I got sucked into that feeling. A shared understanding." I continue to stare at Jejune, processing her words. "Because of that, I embraced them but ignored you, and for that, I'm sorry. Does that make sense?" she asks, finally turning to look at me.

"It does," I quietly respond. Surrounding yourself in a particular environment can impact you in ways you do not know. I did not realize how naïve I was when encompassed in the Amella bubble. Jejune is self aware enough to realize her own behavior being influenced; I wish I was too.

"I gave up once," she exhales. "Turning thirteen, with no parents, left with a new born baby, not ideal," she frowns with a chuckle. A seriousness washes over Jejune's face, erasing her laughter. "I took a knife and locked myself in the bathroom. The knife already cut out my first sphere, and that's when I heard Stevey cry." Shocked, I study Jejune's face as she opens up. My body swims with nerves because although it is finally happening, I can tell this is not easy for Jejune to say. "Man, it hurt like a bitch," she scoffs. "I cut way too deep resulting in the permanent damage, but when I heard Stevey cry, that was more painful. He was crying for someone, anyone, and then it hit me. He was crying for me." Looking to the sky, Jejune closes her eyes. "Apart from that ceremony I haven't cried in front of Stevey. I could never, I had to be invincible. Show him I'm the person to solve all his problems." Jejune looks to me, her emerald eyes glossy. "I know I'm not perfect," she smirks, a slight quiver in her voice. "But I'd like to think I did a good job."

For the first time in a long time, Jejune really looks at me. Clenching her jaw, she blinks rapidly, stopping tears from spilling onto her face. My face grows hot as pressure forms behind my own eyes. She had to raise a child when she was just a child herself. If that is not strength, then I do not know what is.

"You raised a great little man Jejune." Struggling, I sniffle as wetness fills my nostrils. "Your dad would be proud." Jejune closes her eyes, allowing her tears to flow freely.

"I'd like to think so." Without hesitation, I lunge into her. Embracing one another, we well with emotion, each for different reasons. Jejune for the life she has had to endure, and myself for confirming this was worth the risk. It was not false hope to come on this camping trip and extend my stay away from my parents. I squeeze my arms around Jejune, knowing how bittersweet this moment is. Knowing how hard I have tried to get my best friend back. Now that I have got her back, it is going to be even more painful to let her go.

"JJ!"

Interrupting our session of vulnerability, Jejune and I release from one another, speedily composing ourselves.

"Yes baby," Jejune yells back.

"I can't find any sea shells," he sulks, hanging his head low.

"We will help." Jejune reaches into her bag. "You still cool with this?"

"Yeah, it is fine," I reply. Jejune and I splash through the water, joining Stevey in his hunt for shells. Jejune winks and I nod back, initiating our plan. "Have you checked here Stevey?" I ask, walking away from Jejune.

"I already did," he pouts, dragging his feet towards me. Glancing over Stevey's shoulder, Jejune smoothly slides her hand into her pocket like a snake. Soundlessly, Jejune removes a shell, carefully placing it down.

"I think there may be some over here," Jejune sings, swiftly kicking rocks into the air.

"Really!" Stevey shouts, running to the other side. I follow Stevey as he rushes towards Jejune, skidding to a halt. He loudly gasps as he kneels down, brushing away the rocks Jejune kicked. "I found one!"

"Good job little man," Jejune smiles, rubbing his head as he stands. Beaming, he holds the sea shell in the air, presenting it to Jejune and I.

"I can't wait to show my friends!" he squeals.

As Stevey jumps with excitement, Jejune and I share a smile. Being nowhere near the sea, we knew that Stevey would never find any 'sea' shells here. When Jejune asked if she could borrow one I got from the ocean, how could I say no. What I said earlier was true. From stolen sugar cookies, to piggy back rides, to hiding sea shells, Jejune's dad would be more than proud of everything she has done for Stevey.

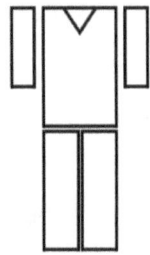

Day three. The final day of our camping trip. As much as I want to enjoy the scenery and live in this moment, the idea of leaving this place lingers over me. Skating across the water, the mountains loom overhead, closing in more and more, suffocating me with the decision I have made.

Before heading back to the living quarters, we stop at the balcony lookout. With no curfew to worry about, we watch the sun disappear behind the jagged rocks, hypnotized by the beautiful sky. With the sun gone, we slowly and carefully make our return down the trail in the dark.

"That's where Rose and I got syrup!" Stevey points as we pass by Cali's trees. Through staggered breaths, we all look to the small wooded area. "Maybe next birthday I can have a syrup cake."

"A syrup cake," Jejune laughs. "I think that might be too sticky."

"Next year I can have a syrup cake and get my makeup like all my friends!" Confused, I look to Jejune and Stevey as they swing their held hand back and forth. Taking notice of my expression, Jejune whispers towards me.

"I promised him when he's ten he can get his dark makeup."

A sadness hits me as I hear her words. So she is planning on staying here. Stumbling, I realize we have reached Cali's flat surface. Jejune stops dead in her tracks as she stares ahead. Following her gaze, I see three people wrestling before the path to the living quarters.

"Stay behind me," Jejune firmly states to Stevey. Cautiously, we make our way to the situation up ahead. Squinting, I try to make out who we are confronting, but the dim lantern lighting and twilight sky show the three people as shadows.

"Over here, over here," Cali says, dragging someone towards the ceremony area. Heart pounding, Jejune, Stevey, and I approach. We wait behind Cali and Wila, both holding a man in their arms. I have never seen this man before. Judging by his clothing and Cali and Wila's concerned states, he looks to be a newcomer.

"Everything okay?" Jejune loudly asks. Cali and Wila turn around, remaining frozen with the man in their arms. In clear view now, I look to the man. It is obvious he is not well. He struggles to breathe, head bobbing up and down, slipping in and out of consciousness. Strangest of all, he is in a long white jumpsuit, heavily soiled with dirt. Where ever he traveled from, nature was not kind to him.

"How was the camping trip?" Cali asks, completely ignoring Jejune's question and the fact she is holding an ill stranger in her arms.

"I think there's a more important topic to discuss," Jejune replies. Stevey remains behind Jejune, tightly gripping her shirt, worriedly peering at the man in Cali's arms.

"Just a newcomer," Cali reassures, plastering a smile on her face as she struggles to hold up the man. "Why don't you all –"

Suddenly, the man gargles loudly, flinging his head to the sky. His eyes roll in the back of his head, his wheezing elongating into the quiet night.

"He needs medicine Cali," Wila pries.

"JJ what's wrong with him?" Stevey whimpers.

"Boo," the man spits. "Boo," he spits again. I turn my ear to the man, attempting to understand what he is saying. As if startled awake from a nightmare, the man opens his bloodshot eyes. With all the strength he can muster, he stares at Cali, speaking directly to her. "Boom. You're it."

Flinging her hands up, Cali shivers with a gasp, dropping the man to the ground. The man collapses loudly against the dry earth. Shaking, Cali steps back as her eyes stay wide, unblinking at the man. Fixated, my gaze stays glued to Cali. This is the first time I have ever seen her truly frightened.

"Cali!" Wila exclaims, kneeling down to the man sprawled out on the ground. "Oh…" she trails off, looking over the newcomer. Gently, Wila brushes her fingers over the man's eyes, closing them forever.

"Is he dead?" Stevey quivers. Tears form in his eyes as he walks in between Jejune and I, looking down at the man. Jejune hoists Stevey on her hip. She grabs his head, placing it on top of her shoulder, out of sight from the incident unfolding.

"Care to explain what's going on," Jejune demands. Wila stays silent as she remains crouched next to the dead stranger. Ignoring the deceased body before me, I continue to stare at Cali. She is just as frazzled as when she dropped the man. Eyes bulging out of her skull, she breathes heavily, anger swirling in her expression. My eyes flick to her hands, clenched immensely tight, the whites of her knuckles matching the stranger's white jumpsuit.

"This is it, isn't it?" Wila questions, turning her attention to Cali. Perplexed, I glance to Jejune, anger painted over her face as she clutches Stevey in her arms. "Cali," Wila whispers, slowly standing up. "Cali when is it happening?" Cali does not respond, frozen like a statue as she continues to clench her fists. "It's clearly happening," Wila cries. "Boom. You're it," she gestures to the white jumpsuit stranger on the ground, repeating his final words. "So how soon? What was the agreement you –"

"WILA SHUT UP!" Cali screams. Jejune and I flinch from her outburst and Stevey covers his ears, dropping the sea shell in his hand.

"I'm sorry," Cali says, walking towards Jejune. Stepping back, Jejune holds Stevey tight. "Stevey I –" A loud crunch echoes over her sentence. Heart breaking, I look down as Cali lifts her foot up, uncovering Stevey's sea shell.

"My sea shell!" Stevey wails.

"It's okay," Jejune says, caressing Stevey's head. "JJ will fix it." Balancing Stevey on her hip, she hastily gathers the broken pieces. "No matter the time, no matter the day, I will always have my big sister JJ. I'll fix it." Jejune continues to comfort Stevey, making her way to the living quarters.

"Stevey –"

"You've done enough Cali," Jejune hisses. She walks away, Stevey's weakened arms dangling behind her as he sobs, gulping for air as his second sphere evaporates off his face. Frustration consumes my body. Jejune worked so hard to give Stevey the perfect birthday, and Cali crushed it. Fuming, I face Cali and Wila.

"Care to explain what's going on," I state, repeating Jejune's words, a hint of anger in my voice. Wila nervously snaps her eyes towards me, not responding. My sight ping pongs from Wila to Cali, anxiously waiting for an answer.

"It's a –" Wila begins to say.

"Wila," Cali bitterly breathes, snapping her head towards her. Shakily closing her eyes, Cali composes herself. "Rose." She opens her eyes, a smile curling on her face. "This is nothing you have to worry about," she calmly states, clasping her hands in front of her. "Have a goodnight."

Dismissed by Cali, I look to Wila, her eyes swarming with apprehension. Uneasy, I do as I am told and walk to the living quarters. Heading down the path, I peer over my shoulder. Wila and Cali's attire blow in the wind as they quietly converse with one another. Mind racing and heart pounding, I face away, rushing to our tent. I have never experienced night after curfew in Amella, but I imagine it would look just like that. Eerily quiet as the moon shines a spotlight on a motionless person, dead on the ground, with strangers standing over them. No friends, no family, no loved ones to mourn their death or identify the body.

Neither Jejune or I slept through the night. Sitting on our bottom bunks, we both numbly faced one another. My mind tired with mental gymnastics as I wracked my brain on what we witnessed. Stevey eventually fell asleep in Jejune's lap as she rubbed his head, quieting his sobs as he cried himself to sleep. Using glue from her fishing supplies, Jejune managed to piece together his shell to the best of her ability. Jejune's arts and crafts time came to an end when the morning sun began to shine through our tent.

Once Stevey awoke, Jejune knew exactly how to cheer him up. She brought Stevey to communal breakfast to be distracted by his friends and show off his newly repaired sea shell. I decide to take a cold shower, hoping the frigid temperature will wake me up. As the ice cold water penetrates my skin, I am on high alert wanting to leave this place. I do not have a plan on how to get back, but I have to leave. Mysterious keys, unknown bullets, secluded shorelines, hidden pills, and now strangers appearing and dying. My stay here has been long enough. Getting dressed, I calm my mind before meeting Jejune and Stevey at breakfast. Leaving the living quarters, a hand suddenly shoots out from a neighboring tent, yanking me inside.

"Rose!" Wila says, hustling me into her tent.

"Wila?"

"You have to stay here," she insists. "It's for your safety."

"What is?" I question, our faces inches from one another.

"Staying in this tent," she whispers. "You can't go outside today."

"What are you talking about?" I look at Wila's worried eyes. "What's happening, you said something last night to Cali about an agreement –"

"It was a warning," she urgently stresses. "They're coming."

"Who's coming?" She violently shakes her head, breathing deeply.

"Please trust me, you can't go outside." She fumbles for my hands, her cold palms squeezing tight. "Please." I stare at Wila, distress in her face.

"Why?" I watch as Wila's eyes flood with tears. Crying, she squeezes my hands extremely tight. "Wila," I swallow. "Why can't I go outside?"

"People are going to die." Fear floods my body. I can tell Wila is not lying.

"I have to find Jejune and Stevey," I say, breaking free from her hold.

"There's no time," she pleads, grabbing my arm.

"I have to!" Flinging the tent curtain open, I hear Wila weakly call for me but I continue on, racing to the breakfast area. If something is going to happen, I have to warn them. Heart pounding in my ears, I march to find any sight of Jejune and Stevey. My face becomes hot as I anxiously search for my friend. I catch a group of fishermen standing as Jejune remains seated, finishing her meal. I run as quickly as I can, stumbling into the table.

"Yo you good?" Jejune laughs, looking up to me.

"Where's Stevey?" I exhale, scouring the open land of Cali wildly.

"He's at the kid's table," Jejune states, continuing to munch on her food. "Showing off his sea shell."

"Grab him and get in the tent right now." Panting, I notice Forest race through the ceremony area, heading for Ivy.

"Rose," Jejune worriedly states, standing up. "You okay?" My eyes stay locked on Forest as he scoops Ivy into his arms. Panicked, I watch as he sprints to the living quarters. Oh my goodness, something is happening.

"Something bad is coming," I barely get out. "Go and –"

BOOM!

A lightning bolt of terror strikes my body. I have only heard that sound a couple of times, but I know exactly what that sound is. That sound is a gun.

BOOM! BOOM!

Two more lightning bolts hit me, shocking me with the most fear I have ever felt. Jejune too soon recognizes what that sound is.

"Stevey," Jejune whispers, turning to the kid's table. "Stevey!" Hopping out of the picnic table, she lunges like a cheetah towards him. As Jejune runs, my ears fill with the sharp shriek of a woman in the ceremony area, kneeling over a body. Someone got hit. My mind flashes with the hysteria that filled the six ballroom on Counting Day. Gunshots. Panic. Screaming. I am reliving my worst nightmare.

"JJ!"

"STEVEY!"

Screaming above the chaos, I manage to hear Jejune and Stevey call for each other. Another shot rings out over Cali and connects with a person. It connects with Stevey. My breath hitches as I watch the bullet slice through Stevey's stomach. As if the ground turned to ice, Jejune slips and crashes forward as we both watch Stevey's tiny body collide with the ground. Shakily, Jejune manages to get up, rushing towards him. I silently approach, trying to process what my eyes are seeing.

Collapsing, Jejune's knees squish against Stevey's blood, vibrantly spreading over the ground. His lifeless fingers sway in the puddle of blood as Jejune rocks him in her arms. My legs buckle as Jejune uncontrollably wails. Like a never ending rainstorm, my vision becomes foggy as tears stream down my face. Jejune painfully groans with sobs. A deep guttural scream. The cries are awful. The type of cries you will never unhear.

V. ANGELO

Involuntarily, my arm flings behind me. Through the haze of my tears, I look down to see a waterfall of red running down my arm. Vomit rises to my throat, infusing my nostrils with the stench. Throbbing, my arm burns with pain as crimson liquid oozes down my skin. The world before me slants as I begin to pass out. Before the shock takes over my body, my head faces Jejune one last time. In slow motion she presses Stevey's ragdoll body against hers, her voice aching with agony. As I thud against the dry flat land, I finally go unconscious, silencing Jejune's horrible cries echoing all around.

Exhaustion fatigues my body as I open my eyes and look around the unfa-miliar tent. Flinching with pain, I notice my right sleeve is bunched on my shoulder, my upper arm wrapped with a thick white bandage. Waking up, my mind plays a horrible memory. Wila's warning, Forest running with Ivy, loud gunshots, Jejune screaming, I was shot, Stevey was…

"You're awake!" Wila emerges from another room, stopping my thoughts. "I was just about to check your wound." I scooch back, propping myself up on the soft couch cushions. Delicately, Wila slowly unravels the bandage around my arm, the air stinging my now open laceration. "Don't worry," she reassures. "It looks worse than it is." As Wila leaves, I timidly look down, inspecting the damage.

Although a small blemish, it definitely looks rough. Fine stitches zigzag across my skin, puffing with a swirl of red, blue, and purple bruising. Sadness swells my body. Using my good arm, I slap my hand against my face, covering my eyes. The image of Jejune holding Stevey in her arms over a pool of his blood flashes in front of me nonstop.

"Luckily Forest got you here in time," Wila says, reentering the room. "No infection but –" she gasps. "Oh sweetie." A breeze swoops by me as she approaches and places her hand on my back, allowing me to let it out. We stay like this for a few minutes, my fingers and palms catching the tears escaping my eyes.

"Is Stevey dead?" I do not want to ask, but I need confirmation.

"Yes." My face scrunches with anguish. I survived, Stevey did not. Usually

I would hold in my tears, suck up my emotions, but I can't. Stevey is gone. He is gone. Sniffling, I finally uncover my face, my tired eyes looking at Wila.

"Why didn't you warn everyone," my voice nasally as I cry. Trickling her hand off my back, her thin gray hair falls on her cheeks as she looks down. Water continues to wiggle down my face as I stare at Wila for a response. Any response. Suddenly, the entrance to her tent opens.

"Wila," Forest says, walking in with an armful of various plants.

"I'm here," she replies, standing up to greet him. Embarrassed, I turn away, quickly wiping my eyes, soreness shooting up my wounded arm. I pull at my shirt, allowing the fabric to absorb my snot.

"How is she?" he worriedly asks, venturing to the kitchen island.

"She's recovering and she's awake," Wila states, placing her hand on Forest's shoulder. I sit on the couch as they turn to face me. Abruptly, Forest walks out of the tent. "I can remove the stitches in a few days," Wila states, ignoring Forest's hasty exit. "There were no complications but there's a lot of tissue in the upper arm." She comes back to the couch to wrap a new bandage. "That's why there was so much blood. Forest thinks you passed out."

Half listening to Wila, more questions pile my brain. Why did only Wila, Forest, and I know what was going to happen? Why didn't Cali warn everyone? Where was Cali? Why did Wila tell me and not Jejune. Where is Jejune? Is she okay?

"Rose?" My spiraling thoughts stop and I look to Wila. "Do you usually faint at the sight of blood?"

"No," I shake my head. At least, not at the sight of other's blood. I did not at the actress on the stage. I did not at the night crew member in the boat. As for me, that was the first time I witnessed that much blood spilling out of my own body. "Where's Jejune?"

"Earlier she was with Cali," Wila replies, securing my new bandage. Thank goodness, she is alive. "Now you'll have some discomfort but –"

"Thank you," I weakly smile. "For everything." I silently wince as I use my arms to push off the couch.

"Rose you need your rest," Wila pressures. Ignoring her, I race out the tent. Blinded by the sun, I squint as I look up and down the path, searching for any sign of others. Spotting people around the ceremony area, I make my way over there. My head rushes with dizziness. Maybe Wila was right, maybe I should rest. Pushing through, I keep going. I have to find Jejune.

"Please!" Cali shouts to the crowd. Rolling my shoulder, I try to stretch out the pain shooting up my arm. I linger back and rise on my tip toes, searching for my friend. "There will be no ceremony tonight." Others murmur concerns. "I've spoken to the victims' loved ones and tonight's ceremony will be replaced with a memorial."

At the word victims, I pause my hunt for Jejune and look to Cali. As if she knew I arrived, Cali looks to me, her dark eyes piercing through me. Devastation washes over me. Hearing Cali's statement out loud validates my memories. I do not want to believe it, but there were victims, and Stevey was one. Instantly, all of Cali begins talking over one another, pounding my ears with their questions.

Lowering from my tip toes, I give up when I do not see Jejune. Feet shuffling, I jog to our tent, flinging the curtain open to emptiness. I hustle to the bathroom, catching a glimpse of myself in the mirror. Shocked, my dark makeup is completely gone and I do not see me, I see Aster. With one sphere under my left eye and blonde hair, I look more like her than myself. I continue to stare at my face, specifically my sphere. Sphere, as in singular not plural. Avoiding my unrecognizable reflection, I exit the bathroom, resuming my hunt for Jejune.

Where could she be?

I walk through the main room to leave when my eye catches something on the kitchen island. Slowly, I back up, studying the two objects lying on the counter. I stare at the objects for some time, my eyes darting between each one. A JJ hat and a sea shell, but not just any JJ hat or any sea shell. Heartbeat rising, I step closer, getting a better look. Jejune's JJ hat is in perfect condition except for the brim, which is soiled with a dark liquid. Swallowing, my eyes look to Stevey's sea shell. The cracks Jejune glued back together are no longer dried clear. Instead, the jagged glue lines are infused with a garnet red.

Numb, I plop down on the kitchen stool. Surprised to find myself crying again, tears crawl down my face as I stare at the hat and shell, stained with Stevey's blood. Both objects rest next to one another, unable to separate, connected by the same traumatic event. Disbelief swells inside me. How could this have happened? Overcome with emotion, I fall forward, burying my face into my arms. Alone, I mimic Jejune's wails, my body trembling as I cry, and cry, and cry. Crying over the pain. The pain of my bullet wound. The pain of Jejune's bloody hat. The pain of Stevey's bloody sea shell. The pain of the unknown. The unknown of how to carry on following a moment like this. There was life before this and there is life after this. Sobbing, the dreadful realization stabs me. Everything has been forever changed. Nothing will ever be the same.

***

Somehow, I muster my utterly depleted body and mind to the memorial Cali spoke of. Rather than one bonfire, four smaller fires have been lit, illuminating the crowd forming. My stomach is sick as I register the purpose of those fires. My sickness is soon replaced with guilt, realizing Stevey was not the only victim, three other people were taken away. With the dim fire and moonlight, I struggle to find Jejune.

"Welcome," Cali projects. "To say yesterday was tragic would be an understatement." Cali stops, the crackling of fires and soft whimpers echoing. "Survivors guilt is the worst kind of guilt, but we have one another to lean on. To mourn the forgotten. Lily, Meadow, Fisher, and Stevey." Like another bullet hit me, despair rips through me. I knew all of them. Of course, I knew Stevey the most, but Lily, Meadow, and Fisher. I spoke with them, got to know them, shared moments with them. "Let us bow our heads as their loved ones join us." On cue, Jejune and the loved ones of the other three victims emerge into the light. Cali continues her speech, but all my senses except for sight turn off.

Mesmerized, I see my friend, Jejune, but she is neither my friend nor Jejune. Her trademark JJ hat is gone, the floral crown Stevey made resting on her bald head. I know I am looking at Jejune, but she is not there. Her eyes, her face, her entire being, she is… empty. A soulless body standing before everyone. I want more than anything to comfort her, but I do not know how. How do you comfort someone who is grieving so greatly. The volume on my ears turns back up as Jejune steps forward. Shining brighter, the fire shows Jejune and the other fishermen carrying a small wooden coffin. Erupting, the four fires glow as the coffins slowly push into their burning flames.

Not able to watch, I close my eyes. Amella trained us how to deal with death. Coping skills. Breathing exercises. Positive distractions. Unfortunately, no amount of training can prepare you for when death actually occurs. Now that I have experienced it first hand, I argue nothing can prepare you for death. Worst of all, death comes for everyone. Young, old. Healthy, sick. Innocent, guilty. Stevey was a young, healthy, and innocent boy. He did not deserve to die. Time may be evil as Cali said, but time can be remorseful. Time can be forgiving. Death, however, is a different story. Death does not discriminate. Death has no mercy.

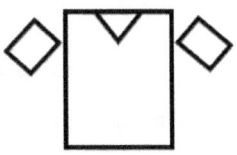

Jejune and I have not spoken since the incident. After the memorial, I anxiously waited, staring at our tent entrance, but she never came. Skipping communal breakfast the next day, I headed straight for Wila's tent. She informed me Jejune was staying with Cali. At first, I was hurt, confused even as to why Jejune would be staying with her and not come back to our tent. Then I realized, although it is hard to stay and sleep in our tent without Stevey there, I can manage. For Jejune however, the pain may be too much. The last time Cali and I spoke was not on the best of terms. Arriving at Cali's tent, I hope she can push our differences aside for Jejune's sake; she is a great performer.

"Rose," Cali says, turning away from her wall of collectable treasures. Before I can respond, Cali glides across the room and hugs me. Surprised by her action, I hug her back with my good arm, letting my wounded arm remain stiff. "I'm so sorry for your loss." This is a phrase that has never been said to me before. I ponder on how to properly respond. Do I say thank you? Do I say it is okay? Do I repeat it back since Cali has also lost people?

"Thanks," I say over her shoulder. "How are you?" Cali releases from our embrace, the long fabric of her sleeves dragging across my bare arms.

"I'd be lying if I said I was okay," Cali smiles. "I'm sure you want to see her." Following Cali, we walk through a curtain and past the kitchen to another closed off section of her tent. Gesturing for me to enter, my muscles tense as I walk inside alone. Closing the curtain behind me, my eyes adjust to see Jejune in the darkened room. The dim lamp shows her sitting on the floor in between a bed and nightstand.

"Jejune." Head sunken down, her floral crown is lopsided as her bald head glows from the lamp. Jejune has cried all her spheres and dark makeup away, leaving only bare skin and her red scar. "Jejune?" I repeat.

Not responding, Jejune keeps her head down. I join her on the floor, leaning forward to look at her. No hat, no makeup, no spheres. She looks so naked. Silence looms over us as we sit across from one another. My eyelids flutter like butterfly wings as I blink to suppress the tears creeping into the corners of my eyes. I have never seen her be this absent from herself.

"How are you?" I ask. Gazing at Jejune, my eyes beg for her to respond. To say anything. To do something. This is not my friend before me. It is so strange, as if I am grieving the loss of someone still here. Someone right in front of me. It makes it that much worse, a constant reminder that a person you love is fading away before you. Squeezing my eyes shut, tears break through my eyelids. "Jejune." Cautiously, I reach my hand out and place it in her palm. It feels like the right thing to do, a way to let her know I am here. "I'm sorry about…" I trail off, not able to finish my sentence. If I say the words, it makes it real, and I do not want to make it real. I do not want to live in this reality, but we have to. "I'm sorry about –"

"His hand," Jejune softly says. Swallowing, I cease the sounds of my cries. She takes a deep breath, her drowsy eyes staring at my hand in hers. I remain silent, allowing Jejune to continue speaking. "His hand was so small." Warmth spreads over my skin as she places her other hand on top of mine. She raises our clasped hands up like a balloon floating to the sky. With our held hands hovering in front of us, she plops her head back. Her scar and bloodshot eye mix with the red tender skin around her eyes. "We used to hold hands like this," she says emotionless. "His palm was so tiny." Biting my lip, I watch Jejune as she stares at our hands. Her eyes dry, my shoulders slightly bounce as I begin crying for the both of us. "Now I –" Jejune's jaw clenches tight. "Now I can never hold his hand again."

As Jejune's words settle, I remember moments of when I held Stevey's hand. His hand was so small, his palm was so tiny, and just like Jejune, I will never be able to hold it again. Remaining in our arm wrestle stance, I bow my head as my face explodes with pressure. Snapping my head up, Jejune is hazy through my watery vision. Choking on my tears, I watch Jejune, her droopy eyes staring past me. How is she not bursting into tears herself.

Not knowing how to handle this, I rip my hand out of Jejune's grip and leave. Blowing past Cali, I send the curtain to her tent flying as I rush to our own. The blaring sun warms my cheeks as tears fall to my lips, my mouth filling with the salty taste. Stumbling into the tent, I heave over, gasping for air. Heart exploding out of my chest, I know I am having another panic attack.

Audibly sucking in air, I stand up and scour the tent. Without Jejune's help like last time, I need to calm myself down. Ground myself. As a six, I never thought I would have to use this, but I am not a six anymore. Amella has trained me for this; it is time to put it to the test. 5, 4, 3, 2, 1...

Step one: List five objects you can see.

I walk into the middle of the room, circling around the tent.

"Table," I breathe. That's one. My eyes twitch to the left.

"Pillow," I stammer. That's two. My eyes flick up.

"Lights," I cry. That's three. My eyes move down.

"Cookie," I whimper. That's four. Stevey loved sugar cookies. Pushing him out of my mind, I blink hard and snap my head to the hallway.

"Bed," I nearly scream. That's five.

Step two: List four objects you can touch.

167

"Stool," I stagger, reaching behind me. I pause, allowing my fingers to truly feel the smoothness of the wood. That's one.

"Fridge," I state, running to the rectangular appliance. I pause, pressing my palm on the cold doorframe. Closing my eyes, I steady my breath as the coolness skates up my arm. That's two.

"Bedframe," I shout, lunging into the hallway. That's three. I slap my hand against the wooden post, instantly regretting the pain shooting up to my bullet wound. Yanking my hand off the bedframe like it is a burning hot stove, I wince in pain and drop my arm down. As I do so, my hand brushes across another object.

"Shirt," I bite through the pain. That's –

I look down, realizing the shirt I grabbed as my object to be Stevey's. I massage the fabric in my hands, staring at his tiny shirt. A shirt he will never be able to wear again. Throwing the shirt down, I try to continue. My Amella training flies out the window as I stare at Stevey's shirt. No matter how much I avoid it, I have to come to terms with it. I can only live in denial for so long. I used to feel a disconnect with Jejune when she would express how much she cared for Stevey, how she would do anything to protect him. Now I understand. The ability to care about another human more than yourself. That emotion was unconditional love. It was taken away sooner than I hoped, but I was given the chance to experience that feeling. That feeling to love someone. I loved Stevey. I loved him and now he is gone.

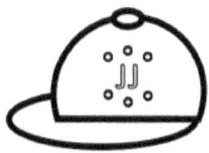

My mind was so drained I woke up not remembering I even fell asleep. The next four days I stayed in bed, clenching my pillow, muffling my cries as tears seeped into the fabric. I did not think a person could cry so much, as if I was making up for all the years I held it in. I guess Frank and Jean were right. Frank when he said Jejune's dad saw the pointlessness to not showing your emotions. Jean when she said my six little dots do not define who I am. As of now, my top sphere holder status is irrelevant.

Isolated, I waited for Jejune to return, but she never did. I did not leave the tent for anything. I know I should have gone outside, mingled, got up and bathed myself, but this was my process; everyone grieves differently. Staying cooped up was the only way my body would handle everything. The second day alone I cried the most. I woke up startled with this feeling I needed to be somewhere, that I was going to be late for an event. When I realized the event I was missing was Counting Day, my defeated body sunk back into bed. That is when my mind truly went down a rabbit hole I could not hop out of. The actress being shot, the map, our travels, Chard, Frank, Fred, Jean, Aster, my parents, finally ending with the looped image of Stevey being shot. The shiny bullet slicing through his stomach again and again. This mess I am in began with the whistle of a gun and ended with a whistle of a gun.

The only interaction I had was with Wila. Yesterday she visited to check my wound. We sat in silence as she removed my stitches and I was beyond thankful for that. As she tended to me in the main room, I stared at the entrance, waiting for Jejune and Stevey to come in. Laughing, holding hands, hearing his tiny footsteps as he giggled. Watching him adjust his glasses beaming with a smile, announcing the latest word he learned how to spell. It was not until Wila left that I grasped that would not happen.

After that, memories of Stevey played across my mind, like a bittersweet montage. The times his tiny arms hugged me, his small voice telling me he loved me. His huge smile with his slicked back hair on Counting Day. Him and I snuggling close to one another in the boat as his sweet voice helped me sleep. His hand sliding in mine when we had our matching hats. His excited face handing me his birthday invitation. His thoughtfulness to put his blanket on me when I was cold. His smile when he jumped for joy finding a sea shell. How he loved sugar cookies, to spell, to laugh, to smile, to hang out with his classmates. How he ran to me and told me it's okay when I lost another sphere. I wish he were here to tell me that now.

Today, on day five of solitude, I decide to shower. I meticulously maneuver in the hot water to keep my wound dry. Although Wila reassured me I could wash it, my arm already throbbed enough, I did not want to aggravate my body anymore. Drying off, my reflection is unrecognizable. My face is puffy from sobbing, my hair frizzy from the humidity, but my eyes are the worst. More specifically under my eyes. My entire life I have had six white dots under my eyes. Every mirror I looked in, every reflection I saw, every photograph I took. Now only skin. Smooth, naked, soft skin. The only semblance of me is my dark brown roots growing off my head, racing to swallow my bleach blonde tips. Sliding the bathroom door open, my ears pick up on someone faintly speaking. Shaking my hair dry, I jump into clothes and walk into the main room to find Oliver.

"Evening. I didn't mean to barge in." Although there is a smile on his face, his eyes are gazing at me with pity. "How are you?"

"I'm okay," I barely say, the first time I have spoken out loud in days. "Do you need something?" The words come out harsher than I intended.

"Jejune was requesting her hat earlier. We're all going to see her so thought I'd grab it." Oliver looks around, spotting the JJ hat on the counter.

"Not that one," I rush towards him. My tired eyes look to the hat and sea shell. The last thing Jejune needs is a bloody hat; she does not need that reminder. "I know which one she wants." Turning around, I head back down the hallway, searching Jejune's bag. Finding another hat, I return to the main room, Oliver shifting in his overalls.

"Thanks," he smiles, reaching out for the hat.

"I can bring it to her." I have not seen Jejune in five days, the least I can do is check up on her. "You said you are all going?"

"Yeah," he nods. "Everyone's paying their visits before dinner." Paying their visits? Following Oliver, we exit the tent. Prepared to squint my eyes, I am surprised to see the sun already setting, a warm red glow overhead. Oliver was not wrong when he said evening. Did I really sleep the entire day? "How are you?" Oliver asks again as we slowly make our way to Cali's tent. "Haven't seen you around."

"Yeah, um," I swallow, thinking of what to say.

"That was a stupid question," Oliver scoffs. "I know we don't really know each other, but, if you need anything, just let me know."

"Thank you," I say. Almost at Cali's tent, I see others entering with various items in hand. Wila crosses in front of us, a bouquet of flowers in her arms. Annoyed, I look away from her. This all could have been prevented if she spoke up, now she wants to bring Jejune flowers; hypocritical if you ask me. Arriving to Cali's tent, Oliver holds the curtain for me as we enter.

"See you around," he says, joining the other fishermen. As Oliver cuts the line, I wait behind the mass amount of people cramped into the tent. Whoever or-chestrated this clearly does not know Jejune, she would not want this parade of peo-ple showering her with gifts. Suddenly, a stampede of giggles files in behind me. I turn to see Stevey's classmates rushing into the tent. The children try to hold in their laughter, covering their mouths and squeezing their eyes tight. As I turn back around, one of the kids taps me on the back.

"What gift did you bring?" a girl asks.

"Oh," I clear my throat, looking to my hand. "A hat."

"You wanna see what we brought?" Forcing a smile, I nod. "Ivy!" the girl says. "Show her what we brought!" Like a moth to a flame, all the children follow Ivy as she approaches me.

"It's for Jejune!" Ivy cheers. All smiles, the children show me a wooden urn with the name STEVEY burned into the smooth surface. "And look," Ivy gleams, turning the urn around. "We all signed it! Here," she passes me the urn. Tucking Jejune's hat under my arm, I reluctantly take the wooden urn.

Holding the urn, my body surges with a sad grossness. Stevey is in there. His smile, laughter, innocence. All of him stuffed into one small box. It makes no sense; I do not think it will ever make sense. On the back is a list of names, the classmates' youthful handwriting carved into the wood. At the top is burned the words YOUR FRIENDS and the bottom is burned WE LOVE YOU. Pressure ex-plodes at the bridge of my nose as I try to hold in my emotions. I look to Stevey's friends, excitement on their faces. They are so happy, too young to understand, too young to grasp the concept that Stevey is *in* there.

"Do you know when Charlie's coming?" Ivy asks.

"What?" I question, my hands sweating as I hold Stevey's remains.

"Do you know when he's coming. We left a spot for him to sign." She points to a blank space in the center. "Charlie is Stevey's best friend and we want him to sign it too. We didn't want him to feel left out."

"I-I don't know," I reply. Not able to contain myself, I quickly hand back the urn and turn around. Breath unsteady, I close my eyes as I think of how kind Stevey's friends are, leaving a spot for Charlie. But that spot will always stay blank because Charlie will never be coming. Charlie will never be able to sign his name or know his best friend is gone.

"She's in the same room," Cali states. Opening my eyes, I realize I am at the start of the line. Still shocked by Cali's cordialness towards me, I swim through curtain after curtain until I find Jejune. Just like five days ago, she has not moved. She is in the same spot, head down, dim light glowing against her head, but this time she is drowning in gifts. Food, cards, flowers, blankets, clothes, a shrine to Jejune and Stevey. As much as I want to talk with Jejune, I do not want a repeat of last time. Feeling guilty, I place the hat down in front of her and walk away.

"Thanks Rose," Jejune whispers. Stopping, I remain with my back turned to her, allowing her words to echo in my skull. Tentative, I peek over my shoulder to see Jejune timidly reach out for her hat.

"You're welcome," I respond, facing back forward.

"My dad made me this hat," she says. Deciding to stay, I fully turn around. "I swore I would never take it off but," she removes the floral crown on her head. "When Stevey died I just wanted to wear the crown he made me." Gaze still down, she secures her infamous JJ hat on, masking her bald head. With her JJ hat on, she looks more like Jejune, the Jejune I know. Deep down though, I know I am not looking at the same Jejune. She scooches forward, finally bringing her head up. Looking to her, the light in her eyes is no longer electric green, the fuse has lost battery. "I promised my dad I would wear it always because he made it for me. I promised Frank I would make my dad proud." Shakily, she closes her dead eyes, tears silently rolling down her tan cheeks. "I broke my promise."

"No," I breathe out. I step forward, sitting in front of her. "Jejune you can't think like that. You –"

"I thought you were leaving," she spits, eyes still closed.

"What?"

"I said I thought you were leaving." Opening her eyes, she looks at me head on. Like old times, her hat casts a shadow over her face, her ruby scar piercing through me. "Why are you still here?"

"I was planning to but," I swallow, studying my friend. My best friend. "I want to be here for you." I grin, moving my hand out to touch her.

"What makes you think I want you to stay," she mutters, pushing away from me. Hurt, I rest my hands on my lap. Staring at her hidden eyes, I respond as sincerely as I can.

"Because I know you would do the same for me." Jejune scoffs, her exhaled laugh a punch to my face.

"I don't need you." Devastation crowds my senses. For a while, I fumble, trying to find a way to respond. Comforting people has not been my strong suit, but I know I am improving upon it. Now that I have, the one person who needs it the most does not want my help. "Just go."

"Jejune," I hiccup in my throat. Pushing my emotions down, I strain to hold the tears eager to flood my face.

"Are you deaf," Jejune exclaims. "I said go." Sinking her head back down, I look at her one last time before her hat completely shields her face. Stunned, I remain in front of her, eventually doing as she wishes. It is no secret Jejune can be sarcastic, stubborn, even down right mean. Everyone grieves differently, I just never thought Jejune would be so spiteful to me.

Not wanting to greet anyone, I detour outside to Cali's porch. Overlooking the swaying trees and solid mountains, my mind fills with the last time I was here, sipping wine with Cali. Her ridiculing my feelings for having no purpose here. Chastising me for wanting to go back to Amella. That same viciousness in Cali's words were just in Jejune's. They are both right. It is time for me to go back, but I need an answer. We were attacked and people died. Jejune does not have any fight in her, and I may have spent the past five days weeping in seclusion, but now I am angry. It is time for someone to speak up, and if no one else is going to, then I will.

"What is wrong with all of you!" I shout to communal dinner. Hushing conversations, my eyes wildly scan the faces of Cali. "Does no one care about what happened?" Bones tense, everyone stares at me with confused expressions. "People were shot and died and you're all sitting here eating like everything is fine. Laughing, smiling, going to pay visits," I state in a mocking tone. Scouring the area, people remain quiet, staring at me as I spit the truth. My eyes fall on Pete standing in front of the buffet, his plate half full of food.

"Pete," I nod my head to him. "Pete, tell them about the bullet in the tree." As my statement echoes over the air, people turn in their seats, waiting for Pete to respond. Gawking at him, I smile, continuing to nod my head.

"I'm sorry Rose," he sighs, his wide shoulders sinking. "I don't know what you're talking about."

"What," I barely breathe out. Utterly shocked, I stare at Pete. Why would he say that? Why would he lie? Out of the corner of my eye I catch Wila standing up a couple picnic tables away.

"Wila! Tell them about the stranger in the white jumpsuit," I demand. "How it was a warning. How you knew people were going to die." Gasps emit from people's mouths as Wila eyes the crowd, fumbling to grab her floral necklace. As her blue eyes look to everyone, she starts to speak.

"There was," she stops, clenching her necklace tight. Exhaling, she looks back to me. Eyes locked, she shakes her head. "There was no stranger."

My head swivels between Wila and Pete, their betrayal like the hardest punch to my gut. Their fists winding up and battering me, rocking my organs and muscles, leaving me speechless. My breathing quickens as I realize it is happening again. Just like Counting Day, people died right in front of our eyes and everyone is acting like nothing ever occurred.

This cannot be happening again.

"Rose," a voice says to me. "Are you feeling okay?" Temples pounding, I turn to see Avery, a smile on her face, her dark eyes full of sympathy.

"NO!" I scream towards her. "No and neither should you! Neither should any of you!" I project to everyone, unbelievably frustrated. "We were attacked! People were shot and killed. Don't you want to know who did it? Why they did it? Don't you all care!" I catch my breath, ceasing my rant.

"Cali already told us," Avery says. "And all is forgiven."

"Told you what?" I state, lowering my voice.

"About the attack." Avery looks to everyone as they weakly smile. After a long moment of silence, she continues. "We know it wasn't your intention. Yours or Jejune's," she quickly adds. "But we forgive you both."

"Forgive us for what?" I question. Genuinely confused, I twitch my head out to the crowd, my eyes begging for an explanation.

"For hiding from Amella," Avery states. "Being fugitives and coming to Cali to hide. We know it was self defense and you didn't mean to put anyone in danger by coming here –"

"You think this is my fault," I stagger, cutting Avery off. "You think this attack was because of *me*. You think Stevey is dead because of *me*." Mind completely blown, I violently shake my head. "We weren't hiding. We were escaping from Amella." I cover my face, a hysteric laugh erupting from my mouth. Oh my goodness, I think I *am* actually going crazy.

"Cali told us it was Amella," Avery states.

"That makes no sense!" Uncovering my face, I quiet my laughter. "If it was really Amella, why didn't they just come for Jejune, Stevey, and I. They wanted us, right?" Raising my eyebrows, I look to Avery for a response. "Why would they attack everyone." If what Avery is saying is true, where is the logic? If Amella truly came here for us, they did not even succeed.

"Cali told us that it –"

"You believe her!" I howl, shutting Avery up. Speechless, I peer at the audience of Cali before me.

"Cali never lies to us," Wila responds.

"Really Wila?" I scoff in disgust. "You knew this was going to happen. Stop lying about the stranger. He was right here," I shake my arms to the ground underneath me, my wound stinging slightly. "He died in front of us!"

"Cali says intense grief can cause people's memories –" Avery starts to say.

"Oh Cali, Cali, Cali!" I stare at Avery, remembering her at the first ceremony. She was a newcomer like us, still brainwashed by Amella. Now we are both here in Cali, yet she still remains under someone else's control.

Looking back out to the sea of people with dark makeup under their eyes, Jejune's statement echoes in my brain. '*We are too confident in what they are telling us is true, and we are too careless to realize what they are telling us is false.*' They are too confident in what Cali is telling them is true and they are too careless to realize what Cali is telling them is false. We live in a validation world, and that is exactly what Cali is giving them. Their painted faces study me, mirroring the same identification. They all look the same, all dress the same, all think the same. They are all one; a twisted hive mind mentality.

"Wake up," I cry. Closing my eyes, I try to comprehend the reality I am currently living in. "It wasn't Amella," I defeatedly say. Although there is a crowd of people before me, I am completely alienated. I have screamed, I have shouted, I have pleaded. How much louder can I speak when no one is listening to me. "Please," I beg. "You have to believe me."

Distancing herself, Avery steps away as her eyes flick behind me. Turning around, Stevey's friends run to the buffet, Cali slowly gliding behind them. Gently smiling, Cali stops, clasping her arms in front of her.

"Rose," she questions. "Have you eaten anything today?" With Cali's grand entrance, I know my fight is over, I have officially lost. No one was believing me before she got here, and they sure will not believe me now. These people treat Cali like her word is law. While she remains calm, I look like the crazy one. When we arrived here, I said this place was nothing like Amella. My statement holds true; this place is nothing like Amella, it is much worse.

Needing to escape, I leave the crowd. Passing Cali, I continue down the path, quickening my strides. My feet rapidly kick up the dusty ground as I run, my watery eyes stinging from the wind. I run past the tents, past the trailers, past Cali's welcome sign, as far away from Cali as I can. Heaving over, I skid to a halt to catch my breath. As I gather my bearings, I realize I have run a good distance away, but not good enough. I overlook Cali's solar panels before me. Standing out amongst the sea of blue, my eyes pinpoint a wooden bench. Sitting on the edge of the bench is a man. My feet step to the stranger and, unsure why, I allow my feet to continue. Approaching closer, I realize the man is no stranger, it is Forest. I may not know him too well, but he is someone, and right now, I need someone. Loneliness has been my sole companion for too long, it will be nice to have other company.

Crunching over pebbles, my muscles relax as I finally reach Forest. He pulls on the collar of his jacket, not breaking his view of the solar panels.

"How's your day going?" he asks in his deep voice. I stare at his profile, his dark eyes stoic, overlooking the landscape.

"Been better days." I sit on the empty spot beside him. As Forest looks ahead, I lean in close. Inches away from him, he does not move, keeping his head forward. Curious, I bring my hand in front of his face. He does not blink as I wave my hand up and down, trying to get a reaction out of him.

"Yes, I'm blind," he chuckles. Mortified, I snatch my hand away. "I may be blind but I can still feel the breeze you're creating."

"Sorry." Uncomfortable, I search for anything to say. I guess my suspicions were correct. "Your eyes –"

"Are normal," he says, finishing my thought. "Yeah." Conversation going quiet, I join him in admiring the scenery.

"This is a nice spot," I say. "Beautiful view."

"Wouldn't know," he smirks. Of course he wouldn't. "I knew once," he dryly confesses. "They are beautiful." Knew once? Was he not always blind? Sunset glimmering off his perfect eyes, I search for any clues of what may have caused his vision damage, but I can find none. Guilty to be gawking at him without his knowledge, I glance back at the mountains.

"I am sorry I took your role."

"Come again?" he questions, leaning towards me.

"Your role," I repeat. "Cali said you worked on the special project before me so you might be mad I took your role." Nodding, he leans away.

"Is that what she said." Forest scoffs, a small smile creeping across his scruffy cheek. "Not surprised. Well just to clarify," he turns to look at me, smirk lingering on his face. "You didn't take my role, and I'm not mad at you." Relieved, I smile, but quickly remember he cannot see that.

"Thank you. At least someone likes me." I look away, embarrassed with how vulnerable I just was. I scramble to change the subject. "Your daughter, Ivy, is a great sewer."

"She's crafty for sure," joy filling his face. "You got any kids?"

"No," I chuckle. "Just my mom and dad back home." The words escape my mouth before I can stop. I swallow a lump of sadness clawing up my throat. Adjusting his jacket, he fidgets with the inside pocket before slapping his palm on his face, scratching his stubble beard. I watch him as he remains like this, deep in thought.

"Second drawer down on the right."

"Huh?"

"Second drawer down on the right there's a phone." He stops scratching his face as his words hover above us. There is a *phone* here? "The key is somewhere on her wall of collectables."

"What?" I ask, not believing what I am hearing.

"In Cali's tent. The phone is in her wooden desk, go during the ceremony tomorrow," he nods. "She would never leave a ceremony, so you'll have time to call your parents."

"Do I –"

"It reaches any phone number." The lump of sadness in my throat transforms to hope. I may have a chance to call my mom and dad. After all this time, I can hear their voices, let them know I am okay.

"Thank you," I genuinely respond. Before I can pry more information out of Forest, he clears his throat.

"I've been on this earth for thirty years," he says. "Been in Cali my whole life. I may not be able to see now, but I can feel that you're lonely." Forest turns his head. Although he is blind, he is looking directly into my eyes. "There's a difference between feeling alone and being alone. You and I," waving his hand between us. "We may not be alone, but we feel alone." I continue to stare into Forest's eyes as a tear falls down my face. "Are your hands free?" I swat my palm under my eye, flicking my tear aside.

"Yeah," I respond, blinking my emotions away.

"I was planning to drop this off at your tent tonight, but since you're here, no time like the present." Fishing inside his jacket, he clears his throat again. "It took many tries, especially in this desert climate," he scoffs, shaking his head. "Ended up having to use one of the trailers out here." He turns to face me, hand still tucked inside his jacket, eyebrows raising over his dark eyes. "I don't think I can fill the bouquet on our picnic table but," he removes his hand from his jacket, his fingers pinching a single rose. "It's a start."

Just as quick as I stopped crying, I quickly begin to cry again. I stare at the fully bloomed rose, the rich red petals slightly dance with the wind. My watery eyes trace the moss green stem. I take notice of the trimmed thorns, a few sharp edges still intact, evident by the small cuts scattered throughout Forest's fingers. My gaze shifts to Forest, his eyes looking slightly down, no longer making direct eye contact with me. Amazement fills me. He did this for... *me*.

"It's dead, isn't it?" Forest asks, face sinking.

"No," I exhale. Tears trickle down my face as I realize I have not said anything. "No, it is perfect."

"That's a relief," he smiles, his cheeks concaving with dimples. "Here you go." He moves the flower forward, extending his gift to me. "A rose for a rose." Sliding towards Forest, I crash into him, hugging him as tight as I can. "Oh…" he replies, fumbling to hug me back.

I cannot put into words how I feel in this moment. How grateful I am to be having this moment. I hold onto him, this man I barely know. Because he may not realize it, but this gesture is more than I could have asked for. We have not even had a real conversation, but he could tell, without sight, that since arriving here, I was in pain. He took time and energy to give me something that, for a moment, would take my pain away. Surrounded by desert sand, rugged mountains, of course it is fitting. A flower would not grow in any of these places. It is a forest that would grow a rose.

Walking into the main room, I admire my rose. Getting back to the tent last night, I immediately grabbed a cup from the cabinets, filled it with water, and placed my perfect flower in the center of the kitchen island. Spending another day alone, rather than lie in bed, I anxiously pace the tent all day. Patiently waiting for the moon to rest in the center of the sky to make my move. The aroma from my rose is euphoric, energizing me with confidence for tonight. At the start of the ceremony, I will sneak into Cali's tent and give my parents their long overdue phone call.

***

Cunningly, I tip toe like a fox, fading into the shadows. Although Cali's voice echoes over the roaring fire of the ceremony, I have this panic she will come back at any moment. But Forest is right, Cali would never miss a ceremony. Swooping her tent entrance open, I peer inside. There is no one, but it is far from empty with the piles of treasures and trash thrown about.

As Forest described, I walk to the wall of collectables. It does not take long for me to find the key he was describing, or rather, set of keys. The same keys to the trailer. The same keys to the yacht. The same keys to the truck. I grip the keys, silencing their jingly tune as I make my way to Cali's desk. Standing over the wooden table, I eye the second drawer down on the right. Looking down, I spread the keys like a folding fan.

T, Y, T, D, B.

T for trailer. Y for yacht. T for truck. Taking a guess, I bend over with the D key in my hand. Although small, the second drawer down on the right does in fact have a key hole mounted on the front. Steadily, I insert the key and turn.

Click.

D for desk. Hand on the handle, I quietly open the drawer to see a phone. It was right under my nose this entire time. Matching the antique decor, the phone is an old fashioned rotary. Not wanting to leave any trace I was here, I keep the phone in its place. Trembling, I remove the phone from the receiver, the dial tone ringing loudly in my ear. Instinctually, I connect my wrist to the phone to pay points to make a call. It takes me a moment to realize I did not have to do that; my classical conditioning kicked in.

My finger moves at lightning speed as I dial my home phone number. Excited and petrified, my body jumps at the start of each ring, the sound elongating with anticipation. If there was any time for my parents to answer the phone, it would be right now.

"Hello?" I grab hold of Cali's desk, my legs unable to hold me up anymore. My mom's voice. It is really my mom's voice. "Hello?"

"Mom," I stagger out. There is a long moment of silence and for a second I think the call has been disconnected.

"Rose?" my mom breathes. Unable to respond, my hand shakes as it grips the phone, like an earthquake is rumbling under my feet. "Rose, oh honey," she worriedly cries. "Rose, oh my, Henry. Henry!" I hear my mom drop the phone as her muffled cries fade away.

"My flower," my dad says. "Are – are you hurt?"

A petite whimper escapes my lips. I cup my hand over my mouth, silencing my cries. Hearing the tremble in my dad's voice is enough to show how much I have hurt them. How much unnecessary pain I have caused. A part of them has been destroyed and I can never repair that.

"I'm okay," I respond. "I'm safe."

"Where are you?" I hear my mom scream in the distance. "Honey where have you been?" she asks, taking hold of the phone.

"I'm –" I never planned this far. I do not have a memorized play by play of what to tell them. "I'll explain everything, but I'm coming home soon." Hysterical, my mom riffles off questions, but I do not stop her. Relaxing on the floor, I savor every syllable that leaves her mouth. This is all I wanted since I arrived here. I thought staying in Cali all this time was an accident, but it was the complete opposite. Jejune always says there are no such things as accidents and she is right. I was meant to stay here so I could have my conversation with Forest to find the phone to call my parents. Back against the desk, I interrupt my mom. "I'm sorry," I blurt out.

"Sorry for what?" my mom questions.

"For not calling," I say, defeat in my voice. "For not checking in."

"Honey," she lovingly responds. "All that matters is that you're okay."

"You sure?"

"I'm sure." I can picture the soft smile on her face. "We can't wait for you to come home."

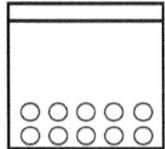

She will understand.

After speaking with my parents, I spent the past three days preparing for my departure. I made a tentative plan. Somehow I would find Jean as well as Fred and Frank. They said if I needed anything, I would know where to find them. Well, I need them. Although there are questions I never got answers to, none of that is important. Where the bullet in the tree came from, why Chard was at the trade run, what the B key goes to, why Cali's citizens were attacked. I have spent countless hours pondering those questions but it is in the past.

She will understand.

Stuffing shirts, pants, and socks in my bag, I convince myself that my decision is for the best, and that Jejune *will* understand. Jejune may be going through a hard time, probably the toughest in her life, but I have to do what is best for me.

As the sun begins to set another day in Cali, I follow the flickering lanterns to say my goodbye to Jejune. If she tells me to go away again, I won't. She may not want to hear what I have to say, but I am going to tell her. I cannot leave in good conscious without attempting to have a positive, proper goodbye.

Upon entering Cali's tent, Cali is not there creepily waiting for me. Finally, I can have real alone time with Jejune. Walking into the guest room, my heart pounds. At the end of the day, she is my best friend.

She will understand.

Surprisingly, Jejune is no longer on the floor. Some strength, from herself or someone else, was involved to move her to the bed. The nightstand now rests over the spot where Jejune laid for days.

"Look who came to join us," Jejune says, turning her face to the wooden urn on the nightstand. Jejune grins but I do not mirror her expression.

"How are… you guys doing?" I hesitantly reply. I regret my words the instant I hear them, but if it will get Jejune to talk, I will play along. Morbid, but I suppose her joking with Stevey's remains is better than her lifeless on the floor.

"I think you know that answer." Her grin fades as she looks to me.

"Jejune." I sit on the edge of the bed. "I came here to tell you I am leaving." With no response, Jejune nods, bobbing her head slowly. Leaning down, I search for her eyes under her hat. "Are you okay with that?" Ceasing her nodding, Jejune picks up her head, her eyebrows disappearing under her hat as she raises them.

"Seriously? Rose," she loudly whispers. "You don't need my permission." I do not want to ask this next question, but I need to know the answer.

"Are you going to stay here?" I have this gut feeling she will stay. Truth is, I do not want her to.

"This place," gesturing all around. "Gave him," she snaps her fingers, pointing to the wooden urn, "what he needed. What I needed." Like a ragdoll, she slumps her arms down, sinking into the bed. "So maybe." She giggles, shrugging her shoulders. My brows furrow with worry as I watch Jejune make a joke of the situation.

"Jejune," I nervously ask. "Are you feeling okay?"

"But," she emphasizes, cutting me off. "I wasn't there for him. No matter the time no matter the day, I'll always have my big sister JJ," she rambles. "I promised to protect him. I promised Frank I would make my father proud. I promised you it would all work out." Another giggle emits as she frowns. "Made all these promises, promises, promises." Jejune looks past me, her scar and bloodshot eye shining off the light next to her. "If I ran a *little* faster, the bullet could have hit me. Stevey could have carried on without me, but I don't think…" she stops, shaking her head. "So yeah, I killed my brother. I killed my dad's only son."

"No you didn't," I exhale towards her, shaking my head.

"I did." No longer looking past me, Jejune tilts her head to me. "*I* did that. Stevey is dead because of me."

"Don't blame yourself. None of this is anyone's fault."

"Nah," she disregards, flinging her hands in the air. "Don't give me that shit. It's mine."

"Jejune!" I loudly breathe towards her. Why is she acting this way? Ignoring me, she repeats the word mine over and over, like a stuck record looping the same lyrics. Jejune reaches across the bed to the nightstand. Resembling a baby with little motor function, she fumbles to grab the handle of the drawer.

"Mine, mine, mine," she incessantly echoes as she digs through the drawer. Finding what she was looking for, Jejune throws a bag on top of the nightstand. My eyes stay glued to the bag of white pills glowing against the lamp light. The same plastic bag of pills hidden in the fabric supply crates. Jejune opens the bag, the soft rustling of pills moving about. Paralyzed, I watch Jejune pinch a couple of pills and pop them in her mouth. Finally coming back to reality, I freak out.

"Jejune, what are you doing!" As I stand to take the bag, Cali comes into the room, plate of food in hand. Blocking the way, Cali tosses the plate on the nightstand and grabs my shoulders, pushing me back.

"Leave her be," Cali calmly states, escorting me out of the tent.

"What is that!" I yell, jumping to look over Cali's shoulder as Jejune palms more pills. Forcibly, Cali makes a turn, leading us both outside to her porch. "What is that!" I furiously shout. "Are you drugging her?"

"No," Cali takes her hands off me. "Just a sedative to ease the pain."

"A sedative?" Disgust fills my voice. She does not need a sedative. "Let me back in!" I march towards Cali.

"I don't think Jejune needs anything to remind her of Stevey right now." Gently smiling, Cali turns around, making her way back into the tent.

"What are you –"

"Just," Cali bites through her teeth, back turned to me. "Leave her be. Let her grieve on her own." Enraged, my breath loudly pushes through my nostrils. This is not Cali's place. Cali does not get to dictate how Jejune grieves or who Jejune gets to see. Furious, I yell at the top of my lungs.

"How is she supposed to grieve if you're drugging her up!"

"She asked for them!" Cali firmly states, turning to face me. A gust of wind blows the anger out of me.

"What?" The rage in my voice vanishes. "No, Jejune would never."

"I offered and she accepted." My eyes sting with sadness. "It's helping her with the pain. She may be strong but," Cali looks to me sympathetically. "Everyone has a point where they need outside help." Shattered, I look down. Not Jejune, she is stronger than that. "Rose." Grabbing my attention, I look back up. Cali's dark eyes glare at me, her ever familiar smile creasing her slim cheekbones. "We are all her friends and we all want JJ to get better."

My bones stiffen. No one calls Jejune JJ except for Stevey. I am suddenly struck with clarity as the veil in front of me is lifted. That first morning, the way Cali's eyes changed when she saw my true face. It may have been subtle, but I still caught it. Since that moment, the dominos have been falling one after the other. Judging my spheres, pitying my occupation, criticizing my purpose. She preaches about all of Cali being equal. Covering our spheres to show our status does not define us. Propagandizing her motto. Vanish your spheres, welcome your tears. But we are not equal. With me around, she knew I would be a disruption. With me around, she knew she would have to work harder to maintain what she loves most: order. The moment she saw I was a top sphere holder, she loathed me. Nothing is more deadly than a jealous girl.

"Are you happy?" I chuckle. Cali stops, looking over her shoulder. Scowling, I stare at her dark eyes behind her blowing hair. "You got what you wanted." Intrigued, Cali fully turns around, clasping her hands in front of her. I scoff, shaking my head. She never wanted me on the special project to gain trust. She wanted to keep me close so she could control me. She is a black widow who spun her web around me. She got me to open up, confide in her, trust her. Creating a false web of security so I would not see the kill coming. How could I not see it sooner? "You'll never have to see me again because I'm leaving. I won't disturb your precious civilization you've created." I watch Cali's eyes intoxicated with power, more specifically, the power she holds over me. Signaling she is done with me, she pivots back to the tent. "I made a phone call to my parents." With this comment, she freezes.

"You what?"

"I found your phone and I called." Now who is the one with the power. "Told them where I am, what's been happening, everything."

"When did you call," Cali asks, rushing to meet me.

"Why does that –"

"When did you call," she asks again, tone serious. The power in her eyes is replaced with panic.

"During the ceremony."

"Three days ago?" Cali questions, her eyes longing for an answer. Hurriedly, I count back the days in my brain.

"Was the ceremony three days ago?"

"Yes," she hastily replies.

"Then yeah," I nod. "Three days ago." Fluttering her eyes closed, Cali inhales deeply.

"Rose you have no idea what you've done." Similar to the night the stranger in the white jumpsuit arrived, Cali is visibly shaken.

"You left me no choice," I defend.

"Rose." Cali opens her eyes, her wide sockets bulging out at me. "Do you have more weapons on you?"

"What?"

"When you came here, Jejune gave me a knife." She nods and I nod back, showing I follow. "You admitted you killed crew members and I don't think you would be brainless enough to leave guns at the scene of a crime. So, I am going to ask you again, do you have more weapons?"

"Why should –"

"You won't be in trouble," Cali hisses. She raises her arms, hands clenched tight into fists. "Please Rose," her bawled up fists vibrating. "Please just answer me." Face swimming with heat, I avoid staring at Cali's red and white knuckles.

"Yes." Softening her grip, she releases her knuckles from their tight hold, her fingers slowly uncurling.

"How many guns do you have?" she asks, lowering her hands.

"Two."

"Keep them loaded." Cali's pale face beams off the moonlight. Processing her words, I fidget for an explanation as she makes her way inside.

"What do you mean?" I call to her. "Are we in danger?"

"No," she laughs hysterically, back still turned to me. "Far worse than that."

Cali's words pulsate my skull along with the heartbeat pounding in my temples. *'Far worse than that.'* My feet disrupt the quiet night air as I race to the tent. What could be far worse than danger? Starting from the far end of the tent, I begin my search in the bathroom. Storage, shower, toilet, sink, cabinets. Nothing. I move into the hallway. I flip the mattresses over, fling the comforters off, feel under the bedframe supports. Nothing. Hurriedly, I run into the kitchen. Cabinets, fridge, sink. Nothing. I continue this behavior, trashing the tent like a wild animal. I circle around the mess I have made. Where could Jejune have hid them? Regret throbs my bullet wound; I should have taken it easier. Clenching my arm, I wince at the ceiling.

I stare at the string lights overhead. My gaze focuses on the electric cord like a cat following a laser pointer. Reaching the corner of the tent, the cord takes a sharp turn towards the floor, disappearing behind a potted plant. Releasing the grip on my arm, I weave through the disassembled couch and debris. Crouching down, I drag the dense potted plant, a chunk of soil spilling out in the process. Expecting the cord to run outside the tent, the cord does the opposite, snaking its way further inside. Instead of traveling to the solar panels, the cord travels under the ginormous area rug.

On hands and knees, I press my cheek flush against the soft carpet. Barely noticeable, my fingers trace the outline of the cord until they bump into the back of the couch. Jumping up, I move all the furniture off the rug. Arm screaming in pain, I pull the couch, shimmy the wooden dining table, and rearrange the entire room.

With the rug clear, I grab the edge and begin rolling, the carpet acting like loose dough forming a cinnamon roll. Halfway through rolling, the cord vanishes again, this time into a square metal door.

Dropping the rug, the bulky fabric thuds to the ground, sending a mist of dusty sand into the air. Although small, the gray sleekness of the door is not hard to miss. My knees press into the hard ground as I hook my finger in the latch. Flinging the door open, the lights above reveal the contents inside.

NO!

Face staring down into the underground box, I remain frozen like a statue. Dread pinches me head to toe painfully slow, as if my body wants me to feel every ounce of terror twisting each and every nerve, muscle, and bone. Blinking hard, I strain my face, hoping when I open them, I will see something different. Blame my mind for simply playing a trick on me. When I eventually relax and open my eyes, I know what I am looking at is real.

Shoved into the bottom of the box are both the guns. I should be elated to have found the guns' hiding spot, but I am the furthest thing from that. Because on top of the guns rest a singular battery pack. This battery pack is what the cord is connected to, what the lights above are connected to, what Cali's lights are connected to. Plain in the center reads *PROPERTY OF* with a logo underneath. An identifier of where the energy needed to power these lights is coming from. I would recognize this logo anywhere. It is a logo I have seen more times than I can count. Three arching white circles on the top and three arching white circles on the bottom surround one word: Amella.

After furiously searching our tent, my wound reopened. As my arm sways back and forth, my wound stings against the tight bandage I hastily wrapped. It is late, easily past midnight. Past the point of caring, I strut to Cali's tent, swinging both guns in my hands. Cali nowhere in sight, I enter Jejune's room to see her passed out on top of the covers. Standing over her I slam the guns on the nightstand. Tears in my eyes, I watch as she groggily wakes up.

"You knew?" I ask. Evident she has taken more pills, she struggles to rub her eyes. I swallow, trying not to choke on my words. "All this time you knew?" Stretching her eyelids, she looks to the guns, pupils so large the green in her eyes is a thin ring.

"Since night one," she mumbles, flopping her head into the pillow. Hearing Jejune's words, all of her actions make sense.

"That's why you didn't sleep the first night we got here." She closes her eyes, nodding her head. "That's why you questioned Cali so hard on the solar panels." Again, she nods her head. It all makes sense. Why she decided the food was no longer poisoned so quickly. Why she said she didn't leave anything behind because she knew. We never left. I have been trying to convince her what this place truly was, but she already knew. "Why didn't you tell me?" Jejune stops nodding, pressing her hands on the sides of her hat.

"Because we failed." She exhales, opening her eyes to the ceiling. Looking at Jejune, it is then I realize how selfish I have been. I was too wrapped up in my own shit to see. Since arriving here, Jejune has been hurting just as much as me.

"We tried to find a better place, but the thing is," she closes her eyes, a single tear escaping out the corner. "There is no better place, Rose. It's all the same." She brings her hands down, keeping her eyes closed. "Amella is everywhere," she eerily sings.

All this time, I thought we escaped Amella. Our excitement to actually change something in our lives. Break the routines, start a new life, put an end to the control. We wanted to take down an empire... but we never left. We have been in the empire this whole time without even a chance to start the crumble. Jolting me out of my depressed state, Jejune giggles, smirking as tears continue to dampen her face.

"Why did you stay?" I weakly ask. "If you knew this whole time, why stay here?" Her giggling stops, silence filling the space between us. Her smirk grows into a wide smile, crinkling the skin surrounding her scar.

"Because Stevey was happy." I close my eyes. Hearing that word: was. Referring to Stevey in the past tense. I know it is true, but, I am not used to it yet. As I open my eyes, Jejune reaches into the nightstand, grabbing the bag of pills. She plops back down into the bed, resting the bag on her lap.

"Stop that!" I demand, lunging towards her. While Jejune swings the bag out of my grasp, a thundering explosion sounds outside. Eyes drooping, Jejune merely shrugs at the noise. A sharp scream reaches my ear from outside. Worry filling my body, I run out of the tent.

At first, I think an illusion is happening. Contrast with the night sky above, a blaring light like the morning sun twinkles at the end of the path. Cautiously, I walk, another scream in the distance making me stop. Concerned, I pick up my pace as a person bolts across the breakfast area. That is when the heat hits me. Exiting the living quarters, I turn to my right to see it is not the sun that is blaring, but a massive fire. The flames rush across the landscape like a tsunami, swallowing the corn field and work stations. Chaos continues as I stare at the orange flames spitting and hissing. As Cali's citizens wiz past me, someone bumps into my shoulder, the immediate pain initiating my fight or flight mode. Clenching my wound, I run faster than I ever have back to the tent.

"Jejune!" I claw my way through each curtain. "We have to go!" Head slumped, the bag of pills rests on her chest, rising and falling as she breathes. "Wake up!" I grab her shoulders, violently shaking her. Her head bobs up and down, her eyes slipping in and out of consciousness. "Jejune!"

"Rose!" a voice states behind me. I turn to see Forest, a mix of anger and panic in his face. "You have to leave, now."

"I can't leave her." I realize I am crying. "I can't leave Jejune."

"I'll get her to safety," Forest reassures. "Take these and go." He throws his hand out, clutching the set of keys. "Take the truck and –"

"I can't leave her!" I shout, distress in my voice. "She's not right –"

"You have to go," he insists, his hand with the keys unwavering. "It's going to be a blood bath." Vision blurry, I look in Forest's eyes. As another scream echoes outside, Cali's manic laugh and words replay in my head.

'Far worse than that.'

"Did you know this would happen?" He does not answer me. "Is that why you told me to make a phone call?" Keeping his hand steady, he flicks his eyes down. Although blind, I know Forest can tell I am staring directly at him. "Forest," I ask, my voice serious. "How did you become blind?"

"Please," he begs, keeping his eyes down. "I would leave myself but," pain scrunches his face as he shakes his head. "You have a chance Rose," he looks up, thrusting his hand out again. "I'm giving you a chance to get out, to see your family, so please take it!" Heart pounding, my body convulses with a whirl of emotions. I snap my head to Jejune, looking to my friend passed out.

She will understand.

My cries mix with the wails of terror outside as I turn to Forest. I know I should be happy. I have a chance to see my mom and dad after all this time. In doing so, I have to leave Jejune. It is beyond cruel, knowing the best decision for me means I have to leave someone I love so much behind.

"Okay. Give me a minute." Forest nods as I run past him. Exiting the tent, my senses fully take in the severity of the situation. The air is hot and my lungs struggle as thick smoke blows everywhere. Reaching our tent, I rush to the hallway, slinging my bag over my back. Ears engulfing with cries for help, my eyes look to the kitchen island. My hands grab Jejune's JJ hat, Stevey's sea shell, and my rose; I will not let these burn to ashes.

Zig zagging through the crowd of hysterics, I make it back, saying okay to let Forest know it is me who has entered. Once in the room, time stops, the reality of my decision punching me with full force. Clearing off the nightstand, I move the guns, putting Jejune's JJ hat down. Softly, I place Stevey's sea shell beside his wooden urn. Facing Jejune, I take the bag of pills off her chest, discarding them into the drawer. I sit on the bed, unprepared for what to say.

"Jejune," I softly say. By some miracle, she slowly opens her eyes. Adjusting her hat, she pulls it back, allowing me to see all her face. Her tired eyes look to my backpack, confusion furrowing her brow.

"Where you going man," she chuckles.

"Jejune." I close my eyes. What can I say to her? There is so much I want to say, but so little time. "I don't know when we'll see each other again." I cannot think like that. I will see her again, I do not know when or how or where, but I will. Opening my eyes, I realize she has fallen back asleep. I take hold of her face, my palms pressed against her cheeks. Coming to, her eyes lock with mine. "I don't know if you'll remember this but," I hang my head, sobbing like a baby. I lean forward, pressing my forehead to hers. "I don't know if you'll remember this but, there's gotta be a better place than this, and I'm gonna find it." I scoop my arms under her, hoisting her limp body into a hug. Like I am trying to break her bones, I squeeze with all my might. Tears in my eyes, I nuzzle my face into her shoulder, holding onto this exact moment for as long as I can. "I'm gonna find it," I repeat. Although faint, I feel Jejune's arms lift, weakly wrapping around me.

It is then I know she understands. She is not saying anything, but her hug is saying more than words could express. Her hug is all I need to know I will be alright, she will be alright, everything will be alright. Just how Stevey hugged me and said it's okay. It may not be okay now, but it will be. She will get back to the Jejune I know. She has been lost in the loss of Stevey, but she will find a way out. I just wish I could be here to see it, but I can't. She is always there for me when I need her, but I have to do this for myself. My heart is broken, shattered into thousands of pieces, but Jejune has picked up a piece. This hug proves she understands.

Pushing down the pain, I release from our embrace. As Jejune collapses back into the bed, I stand up, knowing if I do not leave now, I never will. Grabbing the guns, I realize Forest has left, allowing Jejune and I to have our final goodbye in privacy. Reaching the main room of Cali's tent, Forest fumbles the keys in his hand. Sniffling, I walk to him and he turns.

"Go past the trailers, through the solar panels, and you'll see –"

Rising to my tip toes, I fling my arms around Forest, stopping his rant. I know time is of the essence, but I want to slow down for one second because I am scared. I thought my journey to this place, the great mysterious piece of land out West was scary, but now I am frightened. Terrified of the unknown. There will be no Jejune or Stevey on this journey, I will be completely alone. Forest allows me to embrace him, breaking free from our hug after some time.

"Take the truck," he instructs. "Walk through the solar panels, the truck is all the way in the back."

"Walk through the solar panels," I ask puzzled. "Cali said they are a no access area due to the…" I end my thought as Forest shakes his head.

"They don't work," he states. "It's just a façade." Of course they are; nothing Cali has told me is true. "Now please go."

"Take this," I state, handing Forest one of the two guns. Exchanging items, I grab the keys and leave the tent.

Once again my senses overload with mayhem. I stop, watching the landscape burn in a fiery blaze. Suddenly Cali springs out of my tent, eyes wild. Our eyes meet, the fire behind her lighting the gun in my left palm and the dangling set of keys in the other. Screams of death howl over the crackling flames as Cali and I continue to stare at one another. Her wavy hair and thin shawl drift with the gray smoke filling the air. She clasps her hands in front of her, nodding her head, a small smile on her face.

Unmoving, I take in this gesture, watching her lips curl as she nods towards me silently. As if she has accepted my decision. Acknowledges that if I want to go like she told me I could all those weeks ago, that I can. She cannot stop me. I have broken free from her web. She may think it will not change anything, that I will be trapped in the same old routine, unable to find my purpose if I return. That is where she is wrong. If my journey and my experiences here have taught me anything, it is time is limiting. Time limits with each second, minute, and hour that ticks by. I will not waste anymore of my time.

I take one final look at her before I turn, officially leaving Cali behind. Cali the place and Cali the person. Walking further from the roaring fire, I pass the tents and trailers, morphing with the darkness around me. My eyes take in the beautiful landscape ahead. The mountains are just as breathtaking as they were when we first arrived here. Tears stream down my face. I may not be a six. I may not have any spheres. But this is the strongest I have ever been. These are not tears of pity. These are not tears of pain. These are tears of relief. Marching to the truck, the golden *WELCOME TO CALI* sign shines off the growing fire.

Goodbye. I stare at the sign and continue on. *Goodbye Cali.*

END OF BOOK TWO

Acknowledgements

I would first like to thank the brave men and women who serve and have served our country in the United States Armed Forces. You have sacrificed your time and lives in order to protect all of us. Without you, I would not have been able to write this book.

As mentioned in my dedication, thank you to my family. You have and will always continue to support and love me. A special thank you to my Yia Yia for always telling me I would be a star. To my extended family who I love as my own: Niki, BAE, GiGi, Jewel, Diane, and Shaney Boy.

To my amazing husband, thank you so much for all your support every day and believing in everything I do. Without you, this book series would never have made it on these pages. This short blurb is not nearly enough to express my gratitude for you. I love you now and forever.

To all my students. Thank you for making me a better teacher every day and showing me that you are never too old to learn something new.

Finally, to you, the reader. Thank you for joining Rose, Jejune, and Stevey on another adventure. I hope you enjoyed.

About the Author

V. Angelo is an American author. Graduating with a BA in Psychology and a Master's in Education, Angelo used her studies as inspiration in writing *Cali* to take a deeper look at how we perceive ourselves, perceive others, and perceive the world. When not writing, Angelo can be found dancing, reading, and binge watching reality television. Angelo's world revolves around educating, inspiring, and sharing her love for imagination, and she hopes to show this through her storytelling. *Cali* is Angelo's second novel and the second book in the *Spheres Series*. Visit Angelo's website and follow on social media to stay up to date on future publications, news, and upcoming events.

Website: www.vangeloauthor.com

Social media: @vangeloauthor

www.ingramcontent.com/pod-product-compliance
Lightning Source LLC
Chambersburg PA
CBHW050839180626
46814CB00007B/2535